ETHAN MARCUS STANDS UP

ALSO BY MICHELE WEBER HURWITZ

Ethan Marcus Makes His Mark

BY MICHELE WEBER HURWITZ

ALADDIN
New York London Toronto Sydney New Delhi

ALADDIN
An imprint of Simon & Schuster Children's Publishing Division
1230 Avenue of the Americas, New York, New York 10020
First Aladdin paperback edition November 2018

Also available in an Aladdin hardcover edition.

For information about special discounts for bulk purchases,
please contact Simon & Schuster Special Sales at 1-866-506-1949
or business@simonandschuster.com.
The Simon & Schuster Speakers Bureau can bring authors to your live event.
For more information or to book an event contact the Simon & Schuster Speakers Bureau
at 1-866-248-3049 or visit our website at www.simonspeakers.com.
Book designed by Laura Lyn DiSiena
The text of this book was set in Miller Text.
Manufactured in the United States of America 1018 OFF
10 9 8 7 6 5 4 3 2 1
The Library of Congress has cataloged the hardcover edition as follows:
Names: Hurwitz, Michele Weber, author.
Title: Ethan Marcus stands up / by Michele Weber Hurwitz.
Description: First Aladdin hardcover edition. | New York : Aladdin, 2017. |
Summary: Told from multiple viewpoints, well-behaved Ethan Marcus sets off a
protest and leads a team in inventing a device to help students tired of sitting all day.
Identifiers: LCCN 2017002973 (print) | LCCN 2017030809 (eBook) |
ISBN 9781481489270 (eBook) | ISBN 9781481489256 (hc)
Subjects: | CYAC: Protest movements—Fiction. | Inventions—Fiction. | Schools—Fiction. |
Contests—Fiction. | Brothers and sisters—Fiction. | Friendship—Fiction. |
BISAC: JUVENILE FICTION / Family / Siblings. | JUVENILE FICTION / School & Education. |
JUVENILE FICTION / Social Issues / Friendship.
Classification: LCC PZ7.H95744 (eBook) | LCC PZ7.H95744 Eth 2017 (print) |
DDC [Fic]—dc23
LC record available at https://lccn.loc.gov/2017002973
ISBN 9781481489263 (pbk)

To everyone who stands up for
something they believe in.
Keep it up.

CHAPTER ONE

What Went Down

BRIAN

The thing about this, and what I seriously don't get here, is that it was *Ethan*.

The guy's been my best friend since kindergarten, when we both ran into the bathroom at Zoe Feld-Kramer's birthday party at the Great Ape Pizza Company. We were terrified of the giant fake (but scarily real-looking) gorillas that "play" in a band on a stage by the tables. Can I just say, the silverback with the tambourine gave me nightmares for weeks.

Anyway, no one, not one single person at McNutt Junior High, would ever describe Ethan Marcus as a troublemaker. You look up "good kid" online and a picture of Ethan would come up, I swear. I'm the one who mouths off, not him.

It all happened so fast. One minute, the Delmanator

was going over stuff that's gonna be on the test and we were all so bored we could barely keep our eyes open. The next minute, Ethan was standing by his desk for some reason and wouldn't sit down, even though Delman asked him to about five times. The room got real quiet. Ethan said no thank you, he'd had enough sitting for the day. I mean, it was 2:20 at that point. We'd *all* had enough sitting for the day.

Ethan said, in that super-polite way he has with adults, "If you don't mind, I'd like to stand for the rest of class." Delman's face turned really red, and he said "in fact" he did mind, and told Ethan to "sit down immediately or there will be consequences."

He didn't.

Right then, I could tell Delman was gonna make Ethan sit, just to be tough and show his authority, but I gotta give Ethan credit for sticking to it. Who knew he had it in him? He stood his ground. Literally. Said that sitting was really bad for you, hadn't Mr. Delman heard that? And he was going on strike or something. I couldn't exactly hear that part because the kid behind me had a sudden coughing attack.

Delman looked like he was gonna lose it, so it was unclear whether he'd heard that or not. He must've sent an invisible bat signal to the principal, because then Mrs. D'Antonio marched in and sort of took Ethan's elbow and maneuvered him out the door. And that was the last we saw of him that warm October Monday in seventh-grade language arts.

If you don't count Wesley Pinto pulling the fire alarm (he claimed he smelled smoke, yeah, right) and Zoe almost blowing up the science lab, what Ethan did was by far the coolest thing that's ever happened in school this year. He became a legend in less than five minutes.

ERIN

My brother's gone insane. That's the only explanation I can come up with.

I was taking my usual detailed notes in LA. We have a big test on figures of speech in two days, and I wanted to make sure I understood all the different terms. They can be quite confusing, you know. Brian Kowalski was breathing louder than usual, directly into my ear, so it was hard to concentrate, but I was doing the best I could under those challenging circumstances.

Then out of nowhere, Ethan stood up and started arguing with Mr. Delman, saying something about a protest. I almost dropped my mechanical pencil. Let me clarify here that Ethan got a C-minus in social studies last year. I'm willing to bet that he never read the chapter on the famous demonstrations in history, so how could he even know what a protest is?

Mr. Delman was talking nicely and calmly, exactly the way you would with a crazy person. I tried catching Ethan's eye to advise him to sit down so he wouldn't get in trouble, but he wouldn't look my way. Then Mrs. D'Antonio came in and escorted him out.

He'll probably get suspended. What was he thinking? I can't even begin to imagine. That's why the only reason I can think of is the insanity plea. I mean, my brother's made some questionable, rash decisions before, but nothing like this.

The truth is, Ethan's always had trouble sitting still for long periods of time. Mom and Dad had him tested when he was little, but he didn't have ADHD. The report said he was a high-energy, super-active kid. So

Dad concluded that Ethan had ESD (Ethan Squiggle Disease), which Dad has a little of himself, I think. The two of them at dinner? Up and down like yo-yos. Mom and I just roll our eyes and try to eat in peace. It's not easy, let me tell you.

Anyway, ESD's perfectly fine when you're four or five, but we're in junior high. You'd think Ethan would be calming down by now.

My stomach was in knots after he left class. I could hardly continue my note taking. I was going to attend the Be Green Club meeting after school with Zoe today, but immediate change of plans. I need to find out what happened to my brother, ASAP.

By the way, Ethan and I aren't twins, in case you were wondering. Everyone always thinks we are, even though we don't look anything alike. I look like Mom—impossibly frizzy light brown hair, a pointy chin, exactly five-two and a half.

Ethan looks like Dad—tall and skinny, physically awkward in most situations. We're eleven months apart. With our September and August birthdays, that puts us in the same grade. Sometimes good, many times not.

FYI, I'm the older one. You probably figured that out already.

ZOE

This is so exciting! No one ever wants to do anything around here. I can't tell you how many petitions I've circulated to save parks, endangered animals, and polluted lakes. Mostly, people sign their name and move on, but I don't let that bother me. I just have to work harder to convince them how important these things are.

Last summer I volunteered with the forest preserve to help remove invasive plant species. Do you know that invasive plants can destroy native habitats and threaten vital ecosystems? I get upset just thinking about it.

This year, I'm president of the Be Green Club at McNutt. I'm constantly researching ways to make our school more environmentally friendly. There's so much that can be done! Composting, rain barrels, banning plastic water bottles—and the list goes on. (By the way, I'm looking for more members, because presently, it's only me and Erin. So if you're interested, please let me know.)

Anyway, to see someone else championing an issue

that's important to him, well, I actually got tears in my eyes! I wanted to applaud Ethan's small act of rebellion. Which I did. Softly, under my desk.

Sidebar: I think Ethan is really cute. Please do not tell anyone I said that. Thank you.

WESLEY

This isn't right, man. This is my territory. This is what I do. Everybody at McNutt knows that. I own trouble, okay, and trouble owns me.

I don't have a clue what Marcus thought he was doing, but if that skinny dude pulls something like that again, he and I are gonna have to have a serious talk, if you know what I mean.

Yeah, I'm sure you do.

CHAPTER TWO

What Really Went Down

ETHAN

I have a secret. I am a human Ping-Pong ball.

Not really. Just feels like it most of the time.

For the record, the day started out like any other scoma Monday. In a long line of scoma Mondays. And Tuesdays, Wednesdays, Thursdays, Fridays.

Scoma: my word for a school-coma. Yeah, first you were like, what's he talking about? But now you completely get it. A scoma is what I call that semiconscious, numb, bleary condition we're all sadly familiar with that occurs only during school hours.

It's an epidemic, but no one talks about it.

I've totaled up how long I sit at a desk, and it's about seven hours. It's not so bad at first, in the morning. But later in the day, my feet and legs fall asleep, my brain shuts down, and my butt hurts so bad, I swear when I get home, it's square-shaped. So when I'm not a Ping-Pong ball, I'm SpongeBob.

Monday in Delman's class, it was the perfect storm. The classroom was blindingly sunny and must've been close to ninety degrees. There was an almost-dead fly buzzing on the window, hanging on to its last bit of life. It couldn't escape and neither could we. Delman was droning on and on about similes, metaphors, alliteration, hyperboles. We were all chained to our desks, as per usual.

My sister was raising her hand for every question, with those urgent "Oh! Oh!" please-call-on-me little shouts she does. She was sitting straight up in her chair like always. No slumping, no sliding. No scomas for her. Somehow, she is immune.

Delman, in his blue button-down shirt and trying-to-be-a-cool-teacher tie that says LA IS THE BOMB, was strolling down the aisles. His loafers were tapping in rhythm, exactly matching the ticks of the clock.

We sit in rows in his class—he told us on the first day that he's a "row kind of guy"—and that makes it worse. All you're looking at is the kid's head in front of you, and no amount of interesting hair can keep you from scomatizing.

But see, then, it wasn't like another scoma Monday. Mr. Delman asked someone for an example of personification, and Zoe's hand shot up. Delman called on her and she said, "The waffle jumped out of the toaster."

Delman said, "Excellent example, Zoe," but that didn't make me think about personification, it made me think about waffles. They're one of the most underrated foods, really. Once, when my family stayed at a hotel where you can make your own waffles in the breakfast area, I was in heaven. Peeling off that warm waffle from the flippy machine and dousing it in syrup? Priceless.

Your brain does random weird things when you're in a scoma, I can tell you that. Waffles jumping from toasters led me to think about jumping, and how every day at recess in elementary school, all I did was jump off the top of the jungle gym. I lived for that millisecond of flying through the air. In first grade, I counted how many times I jumped every day. My average was thirty. My high, one amazing day in April, was fifty-nine. I'll never forget that day.

Then I started missing recess because, of course, we

don't get that in seventh grade. Too serious now. That led to watching the fly on the window and feeling bad that it was trapped indoors. Then I noticed this little kid outside with his mom in the park by McNutt. He had a giant kite he kept trying to fly, but it was flopping to the ground every time.

The thing was, though, the kid didn't seem to care. He ran with that kite over and over, and after a while, I thought it didn't matter if the kite flew or not because the kid was having a blast just running around the park with it. When you're in seventh, it's not like that anymore. Doing something just to do it. Not worrying about the outcome.

Delman's loafers tapped down my aisle, and it hit me. How come he—and every teacher in the universe—gets to stand and walk around anytime (and even jump or run if they want to), but I have to sit at my desk and suffer through scoma after scoma?

Breaking point, tipping point, point of no return. Whatever kind of point you call it, I was there. It was like I was possessed or something. It felt like if I didn't get up that very second, I was going to explode.

I snapped. That's the only way I can put it.

I stood up by my desk, told Delman I was doing a protest about how much we have to sit in school. Truthfully, between you and me, I don't even really know why I said the protest part, but it sounded good. Like I knew what I was doing. Like I'd thought it out and had some sort of long-term plan.

The room was sickly quiet as Delman asked me to sit and I kept saying no. I couldn't. I felt so much better standing. My feet were starting to wake up, and I was able to feel my legs again. The fog around my brain was starting to clear.

Delman's face got bright red and mad-looking. "Excuse me?"

I thought about trying to explain. Waffles and recess and jumping and the fly on the window and the kid with the kite. I wasn't exactly going to announce all that to the whole room. But by then it wasn't about the standing anymore, it was about Delman and me, and I knew my reasons wouldn't matter to him. Stuff like that doesn't matter to a row kind of guy.

So I was hauled into D'Antonio's office. Just to sit in

another chair and have the scoma return, full force.

Mrs. D pushed her glasses on top of her head and perched on the edge of her desk. "I'm surprised to see you here, Ethan. This isn't like you. Would you like to tell me what happened?"

I sat there. This was actually the first time I'd gotten in trouble in school, but I was surprisingly calm.

She fake-smiled. Said she wanted to give me the "benefit of the doubt" but looked at me in that way adults do, like they're asking you to tell them your side, but they've already formed their opinion.

I almost tried to explain it to her, even though I figured she wouldn't understand. "The thing is . . . ," I started to say.

"Yes?" She crossed her arms.

I could've come up with a brownnose type of reason. I could've apologized. I could've told her I'd behave and wouldn't disrupt class again. That's what you'd think Ethan Marcus would do.

But I started reading the MCNUTT SCHOOL RULES AND CONDUCT sign on the wall behind her desk. I'd seen it before, of course; there's one in the entryway, another on the cafeteria doors, and one by the gym, too. I'd never really read it completely through, though.

> 1. Be safe, responsible, and respectful.
>
> 2. Show courtesy and consideration for all students and adults. Do not touch other people or their property.
>
> 3. Keep our school neat and clean. Trash goes in the trash bins, recycling in the recycling bins.
>
> 4. The use of cell phones, including text messaging and photo taking, is not allowed during school hours.

There were twelve RULES AND CONDUCT on the sign, but it was number seven that got me. Stabbed me in the heart.

> 7. Sit at your own desk. Feet and chair legs on the floor at all times.

They probably have number seven hanging on a sign in a prison. I looked down at my feet, flat on the floor and already dozing off.

"Ethan." Mrs. D raised an eyebrow. "I'll ask you once more. Would you like to tell me what prompted your disruptive behavior? You're a good kid. I don't think you've been in my office before."

Second breaking point/tipping point/point of no return. Two in one day. A record for a "good kid" like me.

I pointed to the sign, then blurted, "Number seven is completely unfair! You sit at a desk for seven hours a day and see how it feels."

Mavis D'Antonio's nostrils flared. I don't think that was the explanation she was looking for. The number seven reference was completely lost on her.

She stood and brushed her hands like she'd had enough of me. "Very well. You give me no choice, Ethan. I believe that two after-school sessions of Reflection are just what you need right now."

Reflection. Take off the *Reflec* and put in *Deten* and you've got what it really is. Who are they trying to fool? Everyone knows it's Detention with a capital *D*. I'd never gotten it before.

Mrs. D leaned out of her office door. "Mrs. Grimes?"

"I'm on it!" Grimes replied like she'd been listening to every word.

Mrs. D shooed me out. "Please pick up your Reflection

slip from Mrs. Grimes. I will be making a call home. I trust we won't see any more of this behavior."

I got up and walked toward Grimes, otherwise known as Mean Secretary because of her permanently cheerful attitude toward students. Her large butt was glued to her chair like she hadn't gotten up once since school started. On her desk was a collection of about ten of the weirdest-looking cactuses I'd ever seen. Or is it cacti?

"Here you go," she said, handing me a paper and doing this *tsk-tsk* sound. "Let's hope better days are ahead for you, Mr. Marcus."

I ran out of there like the kid with the kite.

"Walk!" Mean shouted.

Of course. That's number five on the sign: Walk at all times. No running, shoving, or boisterous play of any kind.

By the way, you know what number twelve is? Uphold the McNutt motto at all times—We Care!

Uh-huh. Right. If they really cared, they wouldn't have made such a big deal out of a kid needing to stand for a few minutes.

CHAPTER THREE

My Advice

ERIN

As soon as the bell rings, I gather my stuff and rush out of class. When I get to my locker, Ethan's standing in front of his. Lockers are alphabetical, so ours are right next to each other. He's calmly looking at his phone. *Now* he's calm?

I grab his arm. "Ethan! What happened in there? What were you doing? Have you gone insane?"

He holds up his phone. "Look, I have twenty-five texts. Everyone's saying way to go on the protest."

I narrow my eyes. "Great, you're a celebrity and a troublemaker. You did not answer my questions."

He shoves the phone into his jean pocket. "I was gonna explode if I had to sit another second. I snapped, okay? You know how I am. I just needed to get up. Which shouldn't have been a big thing, but Delman turned it into one."

I put my palm across his forehead. Maybe he has a fever. I didn't think of that before. I can't tell if he feels warm because he leans back and swats my hand away.

"What are you doing?" he shouts.

"I thought maybe you were sick."

"I'm not sick. Stop looking at me like that, all worried and everything!"

"But I am worried. How couldn't I be?" I glance around the hallway, lower my voice. "What did Mrs. D'Antonio do to you?"

He shrugs, like he gets sent to the principal every day. "Reflection. Two days. I kind of said something to her."

I gasp. "No! Ethan, tell me you didn't!"

"Uh . . . can't do that."

"What did you say?"

"Just, something. Whatever."

I take a cleansing breath. "Is this going to be on your permanent record?"

"I don't know! It's not like I stole the answers to a test or punched someone!"

Brian Kowalski saunters over in his annoying I-think-

I'm-so-cool way. "Dude," he says, and slaps Ethan on the back. "You're my hero."

"Really?" I open my locker and start putting folders and books into my backpack, arranging them by height and width so the load is evenly balanced.

"Erin McBarren," Brian says in a taunting kind of voice. "Always a pleasure."

"I don't even know what that means."

"It means you are barren of any humor whatsoever," he cracks.

"Very funny. And you are barren of any . . ."

"What?"

"Sincerity." That ought to stump him. His vocabulary skills need work, to put it gently. I offered to help him study for a vocab test last year—I mean, he is Ethan's best friend and I was trying to be nice—but he just laughed. Everything's one big joke to Brian Kowalski.

He gives me his trademark smirk. "Thank you."

I turn to Ethan. "Did you at least apologize?"

"To who?"

"Mrs. D'Antonio! After you said whatever you said."

"No."

"Well, if you want my advice, go back into Mrs. D's office, say you're sorry, admit you lost it for a second, then do the Reflection and put this whole incident behind you."

Brian shuts my locker door with his foot. "He doesn't want your advice."

I pretend Brian's not there. "Ethan? Did you hear me?"

He sighs. "Yes, I heard you."

Some red-haired boy walks by and high-fives Ethan, and then his phone buzzes. He pulls it out, looks at it, shows Brian. "Jamie Pappas wants to know if I can hang out sometime. Maybe I should do protests more often."

Brian bobs his head idiotically, grins, and knocks Ethan's shoulder with his fist. "Awesome. Can I come?"

I groan, but they don't even notice. I hoist my backpack over my shoulder and head toward the back door. Zoe rushes toward me, waving a piece of paper.

"Erin! I got the Invention Day form from Ms. Gilardi!" Zoe twirls, then hooks her arm through mine. "We're going to win this time, I just know it!"

"Absolutely." I narrow my eyes. "This year, we're taking Marlon Romanov down."

She pulls her arm away and gives me a thumbs-up, but then her face drops. "Wait, you're leaving? Aren't you coming to the Be Green Club meeting?"

"Zoe, I'm really sorry, but I need to get home. My brother's going to get in so much trouble. My parents will probably want to ask me what happened. Ethan doesn't explain things too thoroughly."

She bites her lip. "Oh, okay. I don't know if anyone else is coming, though. . . ."

"I'll be there next week, I promise."

"Well, I should go, I guess, in case someone shows up. If no one does, I'll start researching ideas for our Invention Day project." She taps a finger on her chin. "I'm thinking something with invasive plants. You know how much of a problem they are here in Illinois. All throughout the Midwest. Everywhere, really. If we could come up with a solution, that would be our first prize right there. What do you think?"

"For sure. Good idea. We'll talk later!"

I rush out the doors and get in line at bus 4. Ethan and Brian aren't there, of course. They only take the bus in the morning. Unfortunately, Brian lives on the block behind ours, so he's on my bus. They walk home every day even though it's one and three-quarters miles to our house. If it's freezing, if it's hot, snowing, lightning, whatever. Doesn't bother them. Which I don't understand. I mean, weather conditions should not be taken lightly.

I slide into the first seat behind the driver. Mom and Dad have never grounded or even really punished me or Ethan before. But as they say, there's a first time for everything. Not like Ethan's a terrible brother or anything, but let's just say he knows how to get out of things. Turn a situation to his advantage. Everyone thinks he's so nice and polite and friendly, but I know the whole story. I live with him. I see what no one else sees.

Let me just say this: waffles.

That's right. Waffles.

CHAPTER FOUR

Quality Time with the Fam

ETHAN

Here's the scene at home. Mom and Dad come in from work and rush around the kitchen making dinner. Dad, a salad. Mom, chicken that's somehow already been cooking in the oven in a lumpy white mystery sauce.

She opens the oven door, pokes the chicken with a fork, then closes it and puts two packages of rice in the microwave. She keeps eyeing me weirdly, so I know she knows. You just get a sense for those looks. I'm convinced mothers learn how to do them right after their baby's born. While we're asleep in those little hospital infant beds on wheels, they get MLT. Mom Look Training.

When dinner's ready and we're all at the table, she does the concerned/confused look. "So I got a phone call this afternoon from Mrs. D'Antonio. She said you received two Reflection days? For defying authority and being disrespectful? That doesn't sound like you, Ethan. Is it true?"

"It's true," my sister answers, maniacally cutting her chicken into uniform, square, bite-size pieces. She does that every night with whatever we're eating. Cuts the whole thing first, then eats. She's completely OCD about food. About everything.

"Erin," Dad says, "this doesn't concern you."

"I can tell you exactly what happened in LA if you want," she offers. "I'm in that class too."

Mom shakes her head, then gives me the questioning look. "Ethan?"

"Well, yeah. It's true."

Erin pours ranch dressing onto her salad, covering every leaf. "Mr. Delman got really mad."

"Explain the situation to us, honey," Mom says, leaning forward and clasping her hands. "What led to your feeling defiant? Share your thoughts and we can help you work through them. Come up with some strategies for dealing with your emotions."

Mom and Dad are very into empowerment and learning from mistakes. They took a parenting class on positive discipline, so they always say things like that.

"Okay, you know those McNutt rules?" I ask.

Dad nods. "I think they sent them home at the beginning of the year, yes."

"You remember number seven?"

They shake their heads.

"Sit at your own desk. Feet and chair legs on the floor at all times."

Dad laughs and Mom gives *him* the concerned/confused look. "What's the matter with that?" she asks me.

I leap from my chair. "WHAT'S THE MATTER WITH THAT? Do you even know your own son?"

Mom smiles, says yes, she knows her own son.

I pace around the kitchen. "Mom. Dad. I snapped, okay? That's the only way to describe it. I sit for so long in school my feet and legs fall asleep and my butt gets numb. Not to mention my brain clouding over in some sort of Kryptonic haze!"

"Kryptonic?" Erin interrupts. "I don't think that's a word."

I ignore her.

"Let me ask you," Mom says, "I'm merely suggesting

here, but could that be a bit of an exaggeration?"

"No, not at all."

"Why don't you try to calm down, okay? Take a deep breath. Let's talk about this."

I plunk into my chair, the instrument of torture that it is.

Dad shrugs. "Listen, I was the same way, Eth. And I hear you. I get it. But it's school, what can you do? Not much, unfortunately."

Mom scoops a spoonful of rice onto her plate. "So do you want to tell us what happened?"

"Nothing, Mom! All I did was stand up by my desk and say I was protesting how much we have to sit. Delman told me to sit. I didn't. So Mrs. D gave me the two Reflection days. End of story."

Mom raises an eyebrow and does a mega-serious look. It's worse than if she actually yelled. I'm sure that's part of the training—the advanced session on how to intimidate your kid and make him crack. She's got it down.

I swallow. "Well, uh, yeah, also, I told Mrs. D she should sit for seven hours and see how it feels."

"Hmm," Mom says.

"Okay," Dad adds. "Wow."

Erin's chewing her little chicken pieces with wide eyes like she's watching a movie. Do you know she chews each bite exactly five times? I've counted. And she thinks I'm the insane one.

"Well, I sympathize with your predicament," Mom says, "but you'll have to do the Reflection days. You did do something wrong. You can't disrespect your teacher or principal, even if you feel the conditions are unfair."

Dad scratches his beard. "I have to say, I applaud your reason but perhaps not your method."

Erin stops chewing and glances back and forth from Mom to Dad. "I don't understand what is happening here. You're, like, supporting him?"

Mom passes the plate of mystery chicken to Dad, who weirdly seems to want a second helping. "Erin, please," Mom says. "This doesn't affect you."

"But it does. Everyone was talking about what happened. People are texting him like he did some great accomplishment or something."

Dad sits back and grins. "Really?"

Erin's mouth drops open. "When all he did was disrupt class for absolutely no reason—"

I stamp my foot. "Weren't you listening? There was a reason."

"Ethan," she says. "ESD was funny and cute when you were little, but now? It's just embarrassing. Have you thought about getting some help?"

There's my sister, with a direct punch to the gut. I pity her future boyfriend, if there ever is one. "Maybe *you're* the one who needs help, Miss OCD. Go to food-cutting detox or something."

"Okay, okay." Mom holds up her hands. "Enough." She turns to me. "How did it make you feel when Mrs. D'Antonio gave you the Reflection days?"

Back to Parenting 101.

"I don't know, mad?"

"All right, sure. Completely understandable." Mom nods. "After dinner and homework, let's explore that feeling more."

Erin puts her fork down. "Wait. Just a second. You're not going to ground him? Take away Netflix or something?"

"No," Mom says. "Dad and I don't do that. It's not effective. We talk. Work it out. Get to a better place."

Erin frowns, and my shoulders slump way down. To my knees.

The only thing worse than sitting at a desk is talking about my feelings with Mom. I actually think, given the choice, I'd take hours in a chair over that.

CHAPTER FIVE

In the Madhouse

ETHAN

This is how the rest of the night goes. We help clean up the kitchen, and then Erin proceeds to study/wail for the next two hours.

She rereads the chapter in the book five times. Looks over her notes ten times.

Wails: "The LA test is WEDNESDAY!"

She repeats the definitions of figures of speech aloud. Fifteen times. (Notice a pattern of fives here? Yep, more OCD.)

Wails: "These can be SO confusing!"

Then she makes INDEX CARDS with key points and examples.

And wails: "I'm going to FAIL this test!"

Which she most certainly will not. Always says, never does.

Dad paces around the kitchen and catches up on his e-mails while I have therapy in the family room with Mom.

She asks me questions like: "What would've been a better way to handle your frustration?" And, "If you aren't able to change the situation, how could you change your response?" And finally, "What are some better choices you can make in the future?"

I often wonder how different a night at my house is from a night at a mental institution.

My replies generally fall into the "I don't know" category, so Mom ends up feeding me the answers: I should stop and breathe deeply. Define and analyze the problem. Put it into perspective. Think of a viable solution. The only person I can control, she says, is myself.

Thankfully, after close to an hour, Mom's satisfied with her answers and signs the bottom of the Reflection slip, then goes upstairs to check on Erin.

Released at last. I run up to my room, shoot some baskets at the net on the back of my door, then flip through my LA spiral. Most of what I wrote down about figures of speech, I can't even read. My phone keeps buzzing with texts from people, basically saying they hate sitting all the time in school too and we should do something.

They range from: McNutt is a jail to At least I can catch up on my sleep.

Brian's all over my spontaneous protest: So cool today. Still can't believe YOU did that.

Yeah, well. Thank my butt. I didn't plan it.

Ha-ha. What're u gonna do tomorrow? Ur fans wanna know. Repeat performance? Or something bigger?

No, going to Reflection. Not having another therapy session with my mom.

Man, u try to make a statement, all they do is give u detention.

Yep.

Sucks.

This whole time, by the way, Erin and Mom are in her room, TALKING. Their nightly talkathon. After Mom finishes quizzing her (at Erin's request), they discuss what they're reading for their mother-daughter book club, how some girl dyed her hair pink and Erin thinks it's *so ridiculous*, and this boy who might like Erin but she isn't sure, and why the pimple on her chin won't go away. Then they launch into a fifteen-minute comparison of different acne creams!

My door is shut, but her room is next to mine so you can hear everything through the vent. Dad's stretched out on the sofa, holding the remote and snoring. He leaves for work at five a.m. every weekday, so he sleeps through a lot around here at night.

I'm telling you, mental institution.

ERIN

Okay, I think I'm almost there. I'll review more tomorrow, and then I should be good to go. I bombed the first LA test with an 89.2, so I really need to ace this one. No, I'm not grade-obsessed. But preparing thoroughly, doing well, what can I say? It makes me feel proud and happy and accomplished.

You know what I don't get? Why that C-minus in social studies last year didn't upset Ethan at all. His explanation to Mom and Dad was that he's not "good" at social studies. So I'm not exceptionally good at punctuation and spelling, but I view that as a challenge to work harder in those areas. Understanding the use of semicolons is going to take me a while.

I'm about to start the shower when I see Ethan's closed door. Did he even study? How could he? He missed half the review session today when Mrs. D'Antonio escorted him out, and besides, have you seen his notes? A chimpanzee could've written them.

Maybe he'd like to borrow my index cards. I rubber-band them together, then knock on his door.

"Yeah?"

When I open the door, he's lying on his beanbag, tossing a ball into the air and catching it. There's a pile of dirty socks in a corner. And some—yuck—underwear.

"Hi. I wanted to offer you my index cards in case you'd like to use them to review for the test."

He squints at me. "You're offering me your index cards? I could get food on them. Or crumple the paper."

"So don't eat while you're looking them over. And be careful. The thing is, you left halfway through Mr. Delman's review, so you missed a lot, and well, you know . . ."

"You know, what?"

"I just thought it'd help if you read over my notes." I hold up the cards. "I have one for every figure of speech, with several examples—"

"I'm good, thanks."

"No, really, I'm going to take a shower, so I don't need them for the next twenty minutes."

He sighs. "You're not gonna tape a few cards to the shower door?"

I laugh. I've done that on occasion, sure. "No, not tonight. I'm sure it would help you—"

He throws the ball at me and it hits my leg. "Didn't you hear me? I said I'm good! Go take your shower."

I slam the door. See, even when I'm nice and considerate to him, he's rude back to me. That's what I mean about Ethan. What really goes on.

Last summer we went to Dad's company picnic, and the people in his office were all over Ethan. It was Ethan this, Ethan that. They made him the pitcher in the softball game! He tried to recruit me to play the outfield, but he knows I can't catch, so I felt like that was just to put me on the spot and embarrass me. On top of it, Mr. Fun and Games kept striking people out.

During the game, I collected empty cups and helped organize the dessert table. Somehow a bowl of chocolate mousse tipped over and splattered on my white shorts. I tried to wipe it off, but that made it worse. Then everyone kept asking, what happened to your shorts? It was terrible.

On the way home, Ethan and Mom and Dad were saying what a fun day it was, but me? I didn't say a word, just looked out the window. Nobody in this family ever sees my side of the story. They think I get too stressed out over little things, but I ask you, without people like me, how would garbage make it to the can and dessert tables get set up? Not to mention the zillion other things that need getting done.

Just once, I'd like them to see it my way.

CHAPTER SIX

Meanwhile, Back in LA

BRIAN

Tuesday. LA. People are watching. And waiting.

Actual hope was sighted. You could feel the electricity in the stale McNutt air all day. Everyone was talking about Ethan's little act of defiance like it was gonna be the answer to all our problems.

Well, not all. There's still homework, getting up early, cranky teachers, gym class (never a walk in the park for a short, nonathletic joker like me), and the cafeteria food, which goes without saying, but still, had to mention.

We're discussing the symbolism in a short story we were supposed to read, but everyone keeps looking at Ethan. Is something else gonna happen? Will he stand up again? Continue his "protest"? Is Delman gonna say anything to him?

But nope, it's the usual boring old LA with the

Delmanator. Today he's wearing the tie that says LET'S GET SPELLBOUND. As in spelling, not spells. He thinks it's funny. I know, because he showed it to a few kids before class started.

"Get it?" he said, while pointing to the tie and grinning like a deranged comedian.

I rolled my eyes on the way to my desk and muttered, "Let's get hell-bound," but I don't think Delman or anyone else heard my crack. His ties would work better if *he* were actually funny. But when your life revolves around grammar and verb tenses and symbolism, I don't think funny is in the cards.

Around 2:40, I notice Ethan squirming in his chair and I think, *He's gonna do it! He's gonna stand up again!* But the Delmanator gives him the evil teacher eye and Erin gives him the evil sister eye and it obviously works, because he stays in his seat.

It's like the whole incident never happened.

Except for the fact that around three o'clock, Mrs. D'Antonio walks in, stands in the back for a while with her arms crossed, then just leaves. She must've thought Ethan was gonna do something again. Fooled ya, Mavis.

So I start drawing a picture of Jamie Pappas, who sits in the front row. Not that you'd know it was her from the way I draw. Jamie's not one of those popular girls who's mean. She's nice to everyone. And did I mention that she's stomachache pretty? Meaning I get a stomachache every time she's within breathing space? Yeah, that kind of pretty.

One time last summer, Gram took me for dinner at Jamie's dad's restaurant. Which I didn't know was her dad's until we got there or I wouldn't have gone. Jamie was helping out. Gram was complaining about everything. The coffee wasn't hot, there wasn't enough turkey in her salad, she needed more dressing. There was even a draft right above us, apparently, but I didn't feel it.

I pretty much wanted to crawl under the table but (a) Jamie kept coming over and getting Gram whatever she needed, and (b) Gram has hairy legs and long toenails.

And now Jamie wants to hang out with Ethan? I'd give anything to hang out with her. Maybe *I* should stand up and protest? Instead, which I find out when the bell rings, I fell asleep. And worse, I drooled onto the Jamie drawing.

ZOE

When I was walking to LA, Ethan was right in front of me. He's tall, you can't miss him. A lot of the seventh-grade boys are still short, so Ethan kind of stands out. Or up, I guess. Anyway, he wasn't walking with anyone, so I took a deep breath, worked up my courage, and caught up with him.

I told him I was really impressed by his protest yesterday and found it very inspiring.

He shrugged like it was nothing and he did one every day. "I don't know why everyone's making such a thing," he said. "To be honest, I just really, really, really needed to get up and that was all."

I touched his arm lightly and got goose bumps. "That's the thing about protests," I told him. "Sometimes, the least likely people are the ones who change the world without even meaning to. Just because they're passionate about an issue."

He said he wasn't planning to change the world but that his legs fell asleep a lot in class.

I pressed a hand to my heart. "What do you mean? If everyone said that, nothing would ever get better! We have so much to do here! Do you know the kind of ecological damage that invasive plants cause to native habitats? What if people did nothing? I can't bear to imagine what would happen!"

He tilted his head, looked at me kind of funny. Which I get a lot from people.

"Okay, well . . . ," he said.

We reached Mr. Delman's room and I touched his arm again. More goose bumps! "Um, Ethan, I was wondering . . ."

He stopped at the doorway. "Yeah?"

"Would you be interested in joining the Be Green Club? We could really use someone like you." (I thought it best to say "we" to make it sound like there actually is a "we.")

"Oh, uh . . ."

"It's okay, you don't have to answer right away, you can think about it."

He shuffled his feet. "Well, the thing is, I'm trying out for volleyball in a few months, so I probably won't have a lot of time."

I smiled and nodded over and over so he wouldn't

see how disappointed I was. "Oh, no problem, it's okay. I totally understand."

"Sorry, Zoe. But good luck with the club."

"No worries!" I ducked into the room.

And in my hurry to get away from the awkwardness of the situation, I tripped on nothing, whirled my arms in the air like a propeller, and finally crashed into Brian Kowalski, who was standing by his desk, staring at Jamie Pappas.

Brian kind of pushed me upright, and I felt my face get hot and my underarms fill up with sweat. Jamie picked up the bottle of organic kale juice that had fallen out of my tote bag and handed it to me. "Are you okay?" she asked.

I nodded and quickly walked to my desk, head down.

All the boys stare at Jamie. She's pretty and sweet and everything (meaning very developed), but think about this, okay? Does she even know what invasive plants are?

CHAPTER SEVEN

Reflection Time

ETHAN

After school, it's me and Wesley Pinto in room 9 with Ms. Gilardi, the eighth-grade science teacher who people actually like because she is a Teacher Who Cares (TWC). Word is, she'll give you extra points if you stay after school and just talk science with her.

Zoe can't wait to get her next year. She told me she's going to ask her mom to put in a request for her to get Gilardi and not the other eighth-grade science teacher (Mr. Berger, who is not a TWC). It doesn't matter to me either way. They'll both teach the same boring science stuff.

Gilardi smiles at me when I walk in, then pats me on the back. "Welcome," she says, like she's glad I'm here to keep her company and this is a special treat. She has curly blond hair in a giant bun on top of her head with a pencil stuck in it. Blue polished nails and glasses with bright pink frames.

"Find a seat," she says. "Did you bring some homework?"

"Yeah." There are many seats to choose from, but apparently, I pick the one that belongs to Wesley.

He strolls in. "You're in my seat," he says while hovering over me with a threatening look on his face. I move. Then he goes, "Oh wait, I think *that's* my seat." I move again. I'm not messing with him. He has one tattoo already (I've heard), plus a skull drawn on his hand in black Sharpie and these hiking boots that could easily put you on crutches after one swift kick in the shin.

He sprawls in the chair and stares at me. I take my math homework from my backpack and start the first problem, but Wesley's still staring like the second Gilardi turns her back, he's gonna spit at me or tell me to meet him outside after Reflection.

"Wesley," Gilardi says. "Eyes to yourself, please."

He slowly turns away from me.

"Did you bring homework?" she asks him.

"Do I ever?" he cracks.

So the next forty-five minutes of my life is this:

impossible linear equations, Wesley's eyeballs, and the sound of Ms. Gilardi's knitting needles clicking together as she sits at her desk and squints at what might eventually be a scarf. Or sweater.

And a nice bonus to all that: forty-five more minutes in a school desk and chair. The only good thing is that somehow, I get my math homework done.

Wednesday, my second day of doing time, it's more of the same. Me, my bud Wesley, and Gilardi with her knitting needles/scarf/sweater. I'm supposed to be writing my Reflection essay, which needs to be at least one page explaining why I was wrong to do what I did. I've managed to come up with one sentence.

I am sorry for standing up and disrupting class.

That's it. I'm stuck, and have been for a while.

Luckily, Wesley's taking a good, long nap. Gilardi doesn't seem to care. Weirdly, he talks in his sleep. Things like, "Get off me, Brett!" and "But I like bunnies."

I don't even want to go there.

When we have ten minutes left and I'm basically jotting down any random thought I can come up with for the essay, Gilardi sighs, stands, and wiggles her fingers, then stretches her arms over her head. “You know, boys,” she says, “I’ve been thinking.”

That, for some reason, doesn’t sound good.

She claps. “Wesley!”

He jolts awake. “What?”

She sweeps her arm around the room. “It’s my feeling that the students who are in here to do Reflection simply need to channel their energy in a more productive way.”

That sounds like something Mom and Dad would say.

She takes two pieces of paper from a stack on her desk and walks toward me. As she hands me one and Wesley the other, she gets this gigantic beaming type of smile. “What if the two of you participated in our upcoming Invention Day? It’s fun and rewarding and altogether fabulous!”

Wesley snorts. “Are you kidding me? Did you just say ‘Invention Day’?”

She bobs her head excitedly. “I did. I absolutely did. You heard right.”

I hold up my hand, hoping to stop her right there. “Ms. Gilardi, I’m not good at that kind of stuff. Making things or doing science projects. I never was one of those Lego or Minecraft guys, you know?"

"Nonsense!" she cries, stamping her foot. The pencil slides toward the edge of her bun and almost falls out. "We're all makers! Science is life! Life is science! Do you see what I'm saying?"

Wesley and I actually glance at each other, and it's clear neither of us know what she's saying. Wesley sums it up. "Not a clue, Ms. G."

"A lot of my students tell me that—'I'm not good at science, I can't make things.' But—here's a secret—it's only a matter of being curious about the world. That's what makes a good scientist." She pivots toward the window. That pencil is hanging on by, like, one hair. "Every single day, something incredible is waiting to be discovered! Or invented. By makers like you."

Erin would be loving this speech. She's done the science fair every year since preschool, I think. Maybe she was even working on her first experiment when she was a baby—I wouldn't be surprised.

"The thing is," I start to explain, "I'm kinda better at

math." Gilardi doesn't seem to hear me. She's on a roll.

"Science is a way of thinking! It's not about why, it's about why not?" She gestures to me, then Wesley. "I'm willing to bet that if you two put your heads together and directed your energy toward solving a real-life problem, you could come up with one terrific Invention Day project."

She did not just say that. "Us?" I choke out, with a quick side glance at Wesley. He's biting the skin on his thumb.

Gilardi nods happily, like this is the best idea she's ever had in her years as a science teacher.

"I got better things to do with my time," Wesley scoffs.

She lowers her glasses and looks at him. "Like glue bubble wrap to the toilets in the boys' bathroom?"

He shrugs. "They never proved that was me."

Oh man, I remember that. Hilarious at first, then it quickly became an investigation and ended with the banning of bubble wrap at McNutt.

I glance at the paper, which, as I figured, is the form to register for Invention Day. It says, in giant letters at the top: HAVE YOU ALWAYS DREAMED OF BECOMING A YOUNG INVENTOR?

The short answer? No.

My sister's answer, which she says on a daily basis: "Only all my life."

Last night Zoe came over to our house, and she and Erin spent an hour brainstorming ideas to beat Marlon Romanov, the seventh-grade genius/rumored computer hacker who took first at last year's Invention Day, beating them by just a few points. He talks to no one, not one single kid at McNutt, and always has his hair slicked back with thick gel. I've never seen him wear any jeans other than black skinny ones.

If you're ever in a locked room with Marlon Romanov and Wesley Pinto, I don't know which kid would scare you more.

"Thanks," I say, "but I don't think this is for me." I try to give Gilardi the form, but she puts her hands behind her back, shakes her head, and refuses to take it.

"Think about it," she insists. "Better yet, sleep on it." She winks and gives me a smile that doesn't look at all fake. "You know, sometimes, it's a good idea to work within the system."

I'm not sure what that means, but it's four fifteen at

last. Our time is up. Wesley walks out without a word, leaving the form. Gilardi sighs, picks it up, and returns it to the stack on her desk.

Then I feel bad and don't want to do the same thing, so I stuff the paper into my backpack and give her my essay.

"Have a good night, Ethan," she says, putting her knitting into a bag, then signing my Reflection form next to Mom's name to prove I was really here.

"Uh, yeah, you too."

WESLEY

The best thing about Reflection? No Brett. And once in a while, there's even a decent kid there.

You know sometimes I go even when I don't have to? Gilardi's cool with that. She's okay, for a teacher. You didn't hear that from me, though.

One time, she asked how come I had a red mark on my arm, and I got weak for a second. Told her what goes on at my house, how my brother's a state wrestling champion and I'm his personal home opponent. Or so he thinks.

My dad's still disappointed I quit wrestling. He doesn't exactly say it, but I know he thinks it. It woulda been good for me, right? Straightened me out, kept me focused. The discipline and hard work and commitment and all that. Yeah, that's what they tell you.

But it's a bunch of guys acting like they're so tough, wearing those stupid singlets, grabbing each other in headlocks, shouting, spitting out their saliva, standing in line to get weighed, spending hours in a gym that reeks.

A couple of them go here. They pass me in the hallways and I know they see me. I can tell. It's the puffed-up chest, the side-eye, the *you're a loser* smirk.

Be a part of all that? No thanks. I got better things to do with my time.

Wrestlers don't have the corner on toughness, you know.

CHAPTER EIGHT

And So . . .

ETHAN

When I get out of Reflection, Brian's leaning against the row of lockers across the hall. He grins. "Been waitin' for you to get out of the slammer."

I laugh. "It didn't end up being that bad. The worst part was writing the essay."

"What'd you say?"

"Just like, how I won't disrupt class again and I'll respect authority and all that junk."

"What they want to hear."

"Pretty much."

We pass the office. Mean Secretary, surrounded by her cactuses/cacti, is still glued to her chair. She shoots us an angry glare for no reason. Then we go out the front doors and cross the street toward the park across from McNutt.

Brian kicks a pile of leaves by the curb. "I hate how

someone tried to take a stand—ha-ha, right, a stand—and all they do is shut you down. You know what we should do? Start a petition like Zoe always does! Hold a rally! Demand that they let us stand—hey, that rhymes—during our classes if we want to. Say it's a basic human right or something. You know, my mom got a standing desk at work, and she says now her back doesn't hurt anymore. She said it's basically saving her life."

"This is McNutt we're talking about here."

"So?"

"Gilardi's suggestion was that I do Invention Day."

Brian stops. "What?"

"No joke."

"Why would you do *that*?"

"To channel my energy in a, uh, more productive way."

"Ethan, listen to me very carefully. Kids who invent things know about stuff like computer chips and solar energy and quantum physics. They shouldn't even be in school, they should be running their own tech companies. You, my friend, are not that kind of kid."

"I know, believe me. It's like she thought I was Erin. Gilardi thinks science is the answer to everything."

Brian's mouth drops open in fake shock. "Wait, you mean it isn't?"

We walk through the park, which is deserted except for someone sitting on a bench, feeding some big white birds. They're going nutso, squawking and pecking their heads at the ground. I can only see the back of the person, but then I realize I recognize his shoes. Or rather, his hiking boots.

I elbow Brian. "Isn't that Wesley Pinto?"

He squints. "Yeah, I think."

"Is he feeding . . . what are those, seagulls?"

"Seems to be the case."

"What's that all about?"

Brian rolls his eyes. "Who knows? He's probably poisoning them or something."

"Yeah, right."

Maybe that's what he likes to do with his time. Without even saying anything to each other, we turn and go the long way around the park so he doesn't see us. I don't need any more encounters with Wesley today, that's for sure.

"Little-known fact about seagulls," Brian says. "People call them garbage cans with wings."

"Okay. Uh . . . why?"

"They eat garbage, duh. They're one of the best animal scavengers out there."

This is why Brian and I are friends. Who else remembers that kind of stuff and can recall it at just the right moment?

"Now you know," he says.

"Glad I do."

We knock shoulders and split at the corner.

When I get home, Erin's in the garage, arranging things on the long folding table we usually only use for holidays when our cousins come over. She's got a bunch of small glass bottles evenly lined up and a pile of branches and leaves. Plus random things like eyedroppers and a plastic spray bottle and a bunch of black Sharpies on top of a pad of paper.

"What're you doing?" I ask.

"Setting up," she says, as if this is obvious.

"For Invention Day?"

She rolls her eyes. "No, for fashion day."

"What's your project?"

"I'm not going to tell you that."

"Why not? It's not like I'm planning to steal your idea."

"Zoe and I are keeping it top secret. The last thing we need is for Marlon to somehow find out what we're doing." She tilts her head. "Why are you so interested anyway?"

"Gilardi told me today she thinks I should enter."

Erin's eyes get wide. Then she bursts out laughing. She laughs nonstop for what seems like several minutes. Finally, she stops long enough to ask, "YOU?" then cracks up again.

"Hey, it's not *that* funny."

"Yes, it is!" She wipes away tears. "Best thing I've heard all day! What would you possibly invent?" She snaps her fingers. "Wait, I have it! A cure for ESD!"

"Ha-ha. You can stop now. I'm not entering."

"Of course you're not." She looks back at the table, apparently consulting a list of items and checking things off.

"I can do stuff, you know."

She closes the cap on a Sharpie with a solid click. "You can. Three hundred volleyball sets in a row on the driveway."

"Yeah, see?"

"But not science stuff, Ethan."

I walk toward the door to the house, then stop and take the Invention Day form out of my backpack. I look at it for a few seconds, then toss it into the recycling bin. There aren't many things my sister and I agree on, but this is one.

There are only two other things I can think of: (1) We love roasted marshmallows and would gladly eat them anytime, anywhere, in place of any meal; and (2) We hate tomatoes. When we were little, we formed a tomato haters' club. It lasted one day and we were the only two members. Mom was making tomato soup for lunch, and we marched around the kitchen with signs that said DOWN WITH TOMATOES! and TOMATOES ARE THE WORST FOOD EVER! Except we spelled it TOEMAYTOES. The one thing Erin sucks at is spelling. Because of course, she made the signs.

Anyway, it's been a downhill ride since then. And right now, we're solidly in the driving-each-other-crazy zone. Basically, my sister and I have gone from marshmallows and the tomato haters' club to living in opposite galaxies.

CHAPTER NINE

A Cosmic Sign

BRIAN

After dinner, Mom asks if I'll help her put up our Halloween decorations outside.

I make a fist and curl my arm, then push up the skin like I have a huge muscle. "Iron Man at your service."

She laughs. "I'll still call you Brian, if that's okay."

I follow her into the garage, wondering when the heck I'm going to be taller than my own mother, who's less than five feet. Dad's short too. The odds for tallness are not good.

I get a ladder and start taking the decorations from a high shelf, then handing them to Mom. One smiling pumpkin after another, a ghost holding a basket of candy corn, and a sign that says WELCOME TO THE HOUSE OF BOO.

"These are so lame," I say. "We've had the same decorations since I was in preschool."

She puts her hands on her hips. "What do you mean? I love these decorations! Each one has a special meaning." She picks up the Boo sign. "We got this when we went to that pumpkin farm in Wisconsin. Remember the hay ride? And the corn maze?"

"No." I climb down. "Mom. These are embarrassing. We need skeletons, vampires, gravestones, blood, you know, that kind of stuff."

She looks at the pile on the garage floor. "You're saying these are too babyish?"

"Uh . . . yeah."

Her face lights up. "How about we go to Target? You'll pick out some cool new ones." Target, her favorite store on earth. Any excuse to go, she's there.

"Now?"

She nods excitedly. "Yes! Why not?"

I shrug. "Okay, sure."

"I'll get my purse!"

We're in our ancient, rusty minivan five minutes later and Mom takes her secret shortcut through several neighborhoods involving many death-defying turns. When Mom's at the wheel, you just hang on to the door handle and hope for the best. Finally she zooms into the parking lot, looks up at the red neon sign, and grins. "Vampires, here we come!"

"Take it easy, Mom. Try to contain yourself. It's just Halloween decorations."

"I don't want you to feel embarrassed. Come on."

When we're inside the store, Mom grabs a cart and we go directly to the Halloween section. She points to a bloody ghost, then a mummy. "I see what you mean!" She starts loading the cart with every ghoulish item in sight. That's another thing with my mom. When she's excited about something, she goes way overboard. Our house is gonna morph from Happy Halloween into a bad horror movie.

After she can't fit one more thing into the cart, I think we're done and heading to the checkout, but she stops at the boys' section and insists that I get some new jeans.

"I haven't grown," I say. Some of the guys at school are already in men's sizes. And they're shaving. And . . . other things are happening, so I hear.

"You certainly have grown," she insists.

She steers the cart through the racks of clothes and I

follow, suddenly feeling like I'm in a desert with no water and I'm never gonna make it out. One thing I avoid at all costs—trying on clothes. I'd rather have head lice again than spend time in a claustrophobic dressing room with a pile of jeans and Mom waiting outside the door.

"You can't just spring this on me," I complain. "Besides, new jeans aren't going to make a difference."

She cups her hand around my chin. "Don't say that. You are a very handsome boy. You know that, don't you?"

If I weighed three hundred pounds and had a face full of zits, she'd still tell me I was handsome. Which is an incredibly strange way to compliment a guy. Hand some? Hand some what?

I move her hand away. "Mom. Please. We're in public."

She takes a few pairs of jeans from a shelf, gives them to me, then points to the dressing rooms. I trudge inside one, shut the door, and immediately start breathing like Darth Vader.

She knocks and tells me to come out and show her.

"This was not in the deal!" I shout. "You said decorations! You tricked me!"

I come out with a pair of jeans on and she lifts my shirt and runs her finger around the waistband. I pull my shirt down.

Mom steps back. "You look very grown-up."

"Good, we're done." I change back into the pants I was wearing, stumble out of the dressing room, turn the corner, and literally bump into Jamie.

Mom's a foot away, checking her phone, guarding our decoration-filled cart.

Jamie smiles her amazing smile. "Oh, hi, Brian. Doing some shopping?"

I stare at the jeans like they just appeared in my hand. "Yeah, you know. Gettin' taller."

"Oh," Jamie says. "That's good."

What's that mean? She agrees I'm getting taller? Am I? Maybe Mom was right.

I send Mom a silent signal to not look up. Doesn't work. She wheels the cart closer and waves at Jamie. "Hi, I'm Brian's mom, Halina Kowalski."

"Hi. Nice to meet you. Wow, that's a lot of Halloween decorations."

I stand there. If Mom starts talking about the

decorations, I might have to tackle her right here in the middle of the clothing area.

"Oh, well," Mom laughs. "Brian felt ours were too babyish. So here we are."

"For sure." Jamie shakes out her hair and I almost lose consciousness.

Mom keeps going. "One thing about the Kowalskis, when we've got a job to do, we're on it faster than you can slice a sausage."

At that point, it's a choice between clamping my hand over her mouth, diving into a rack of sweaters, or making a run for it. I opt for choice number three and grab the cart. "We're kind of in a hurry!" I shout over my shoulder.

Jamie does this cute little fluttery wave. "See you at school."

She walks away and I rush toward the checkout, with Mom stopping at every display and me pulling her arm and telling her we need to go.

"Seems like a nice girl," Mom says as we're finally checking out. She throws a lint roller into the cart. "What's her name?"

"Jamie," I whisper, and suddenly, when I hear myself

say it, I know this as sure as I know anything. The fact that we keep bumping into each other in random places is a cosmic sign we are meant to be in a relationship. Or at least have a thing.

Don't you agree? I mean, it can't be a coincidence anymore, right?

Mom and I walk out, head toward the minivan. I look for Jamie in the parking lot but don't see her anywhere. But get this. The A is blinking in the Target sign. And it wasn't before, when we came in.

The A!

You can't tell me that isn't another cosmic sign. Target sign/cosmic sign. Come on, are you with me here? There's an A in Jamie, of course. And *two* in Pappas.

CHAPTER TEN

The Secret

ERIN

I'll tell you. I can barely keep it in, anyway. Are you ready? Okay, here it is.

Zoe and I are going to invent a solution to stop the spread of invasive plant species.

Our theory is that certain organic elements or natural chemical compounds will be able to, in a sense, smother the seedlings of invasive plants, thus preventing their growth and spread. How brilliant is that? Basically, we'll shut them down before they even have a chance to take root.

The plan is to test several substances, including cayenne, black cumin seed oil, elderberry, licorice root, and tea tree oil. And guess what? That's just the beginning of our list!

We plan to start this weekend. The sooner the better.

We have so many substances to examine, and then we have to figure out how it would be applied. A spray? Powder? Granules? We're not sure about that part yet. But that's the amazing thing about inventions. Many times, you make discoveries as you go along.

I told Mom and Dad they can have the garage back in November, after Invention Day. They weren't exactly happy about that, but they agreed to make a sacrifice in the name of scientific research. I offered to set and clear the table every night. I do that anyway, since Ethan's usually MIA daily at five forty-five and six thirty p.m. But still, I wanted Mom and Dad to know I'll do something in return.

If Zoe and I win and have a chance at earning an actual US patent for our discovery . . . I don't even want to think about that right now. We have a long road ahead. But I'm confident we'll get there.

I heard through the rumor mill that Marlon's doing something with robotics. So last year. It's been done. I can't believe he doesn't know that!

Other than Marlon, I don't think we have a lot of competition. Parneeta's working on a lighter-weight backpack.

Naomi's creating an improved bandage that delivers medicine and won't fall off. Way, way too basic, and not even that important in the grand scheme, you know?

So, NO JINX, but I think we've got this!

Except . . . I'll admit, one thing worries me . . . Zoe's been a little distracted lately. I don't know what's going on with her—she's been spacey and dreamy and sometimes doesn't even hear me when I ask her something. I'll have to talk to her. We need 100 percent focus in order to take first place.

Now, if you'll excuse me, I have to research more substances to add to our list. As they say in the invention world: If it can be imagined, it can be done.

Actually, I don't know if that was ever said, but I'm saying it now.

CHAPTER ELEVEN

The Carrot Seed

ETHAN

That night at dinner, Mom and Dad say they're proud of me for doing the Reflection days without any arguments, and they hope I "learned something" from this experience.

"Did you?" Mom asks.

I push the mashed potatoes on my plate into a small ski hill. "Sure."

Thankfully, she doesn't ask me what. Because really, I don't know if I did.

"I think I can safely say that I learn something every day," Erin says, stabbing a piece of broccoli with her fork. "And not just in school."

"Of course you do." Mom beams.

"Like today," Erin continues, "I read this article that concluded all humans are descended from the same population in Africa around fifty to eighty thousand years ago."

I stare at my sister. Where did she even find that article?

"Interesting," Dad says. "We can always count on Erin for a fascinating fact of the day."

I shrug. "I'll stick to video games."

Mom pats my arm. "That's okay, honey."

"Nothing wrong with those," Dad says.

"Sure," Erin adds.

Sometimes I think they all think I'm an idiot. I mean not really, but you know.

After we're done eating, I go up to my room and look over the pile of homework I'm supposed to do. I should study more, I know that. The LA test today? Not a great experience. But everyone said it was hard. Even Erin. So all the studying in the world probably wouldn't have helped.

I'm attempting to decode a science handout on the parts of a cell when there's a knock on my door, and then Mom pops her head inside. "I'm cleaning out the bookcase in the family room."

Her favorite activity besides Parenting 101 is

cleaning something out. We're the opposite of hoarders. As soon as someone's done using something or we don't need it anymore, Mom packs it up for Goodwill.

"If you want anything," she says, "take it now."

"What's there?"

"I don't know. Go have a look. Erin grabbed a few old favorites."

With Mom, now means now. They'll be gone tomorrow. Unless some of them can be used for therapy sessions.

I go downstairs and see a couple of stacks of books on the floor. I take a quick glance through them, but nothing jumps out. "I don't want any!" I shout to Mom, wherever she is.

"You're sure?"

"Yeah!"

"What about the book on the butterfly life cycle? That was your favorite when you were little!"

"Nope, I'm good!"

I leap up the stairs, two at a time. She might've thought that was my favorite book when I was little, but she doesn't know. My favorite was something just between me and Dad. And him and his dad. It's a Marcus guy thing.

And that book, I have.

Back in my room, I carefully shut the door, then open my sock drawer. I reach my hand underneath the bad socks and pull out the book.

The Carrot Seed.

You might think this is weird, and I agree, it's a little weird, but after you hear why I have a picture book hidden in my sock drawer, then you might not think it's that weird.

It was written in 1945 and belonged to my grandpa, Dad's dad, who I never knew. He read it to Dad when he was little. Then Dad read it to me when I was little. Like, all the time, because I loved it and never got tired of hearing the story.

And let me tell you, I still think *The Carrot Seed* is one of the best books ever written. I'm not kidding.

There's this kid who plants a carrot seed, right, and everyone tells him it's not gonna grow, but he waters the seed and pulls the weeds around it. People keep saying it's not gonna grow, nothing will happen, give it up, kid (basically implying he's a real chump), but he doesn't listen and continues his watering-and-weeding thing.

At the end, it's the best. This gigantic carrot sprouts up, and the kid carts it off in a wheelbarrow. He has this little smile on his face like he never doubted that tiny seed once. Stories don't get much better than that. We Marcus guys know a good thing when we see it.

So here's the bad part. When I got a little older but not that much older, I took a black crayon and wrote *me* over the kid's head on every single page.

Dad got pretty mad. He said, "Why would you write in a book? Especially one like this."

I remember looking at Dad's face, and thinking about his dad, and feeling like I should be kicked out of the family. But I had a reason. I told Dad, "It was only because I wanted to be the carrot seed kid."

I think he got it. And the next day, he wasn't so mad anymore. We tried but couldn't erase the crayon.

I sink onto my beanbag and open to the last page, where the kid has the carrot, and stare at those two shaky letters. *Me.*

When I was four, I had big dreams. And when I was five, and six. Who doesn't? The usual stuff. Become a superhero, play in the NBA, slay a dragon. Whatever. The point is, like the kid in the book, I thought things could happen if I believed hard enough.

I stretch out, cross my hands behind my head. So what happened? Yeah, okay, I'm not a little kid anymore. But when did I become the kid who goes along with everything and gets along with everyone? The laid-back guy who never takes anything all that seriously because . . . it's just easier not to?

That's okay some of the time, but for that one moment in LA when I refused to sit in my chair, it felt kinda excellent to be on the other side. Exhilarating, to use a current vocab word. Make some trouble. Take a stand. Believe I could do something, I guess.

That day a long time ago when Erin and I did the tomato protest? Mom thought it was the most hilarious thing and didn't make us eat the tomato soup. I remember feeling exhilarated then too. Erin and I danced around the kitchen, celebrating our escape from those terrible *toemaytoes*.

I still won't eat them. At least I stuck to that. But yeah, after my brief rebel moment in Delman's class and then mouthing off to D'Antonio, what do I do? I cave in.

Give it up. Do my Reflection time, and then it's back to being the good kid.

And the worst part is, nothing's changed. My legs still fall asleep and my brain still shuts down and scomas still happen on a daily basis.

I close the book with a loud slap. The little carrot seed dude wouldn't have sold out and written a dumb Reflection essay. He would have done something. He would have believed.

CHAPTER TWELVE

Brilliance (I Think)

ETHAN

Later, when I get into bed, I put the book next to me. I'd appreciate it if you don't mention that to anyone. No one needs to know.

For some reason, I start thinking about how Gilardi wouldn't take the Invention Day form when I tried to give it to her. How she told me to sleep on it. I don't know what she thought I'd come up with after a night of sleep, because people who invent things gotta have way different dreams than the rest of us. Involving electronic circuits and jet engines and atomic particles, I'd think.

I usually dream about food. Or showing up at volleyball tryouts in my underwear and without my gym shoes.

Except everything must be bouncing around in my head, because I don't dream about food or tryouts. I have this mixed-up dream with Gilardi waving a pencil and running away from me, Delman yelling at me to sit down or I'll go to jail, and then it's all calm and I'm planting carrots. I'm wearing Wesley Pinto's boots through the whole thing, but they're way too big and I keep tripping.

Finally I wake up. The weird dream fades away, and all I'm left with is an idea. It just comes to me. And it's a way to solve my scoma problem, and maybe even cure ESD forever.

I'm not sure if I'll feel the same way tomorrow, but in the quiet darkness of my room, the idea sounds brilliant. Amazing. Doable. Rooms at two a.m. are helpful in that way. Very nonjudgmental.

Are you ready for this? It's an invention.

I know, I know.

I know what I said, and I know what you're thinking—that this is Erin's department—but guess what? I have that exhilarated feeling.

I get out of bed and tiptoe into the hallway, then sneak downstairs, carefully making my way to the garage because there's not even one light on in our entire house. In the garage, I flip on the light, then open the lid of the recycling bin.

I have to dig a bit, but then I find it—the Invention Day registration form. It's only a little crumpled, and sort of wet from being underneath a milk carton.

I go back upstairs without Mom or Dad waking up, or Erin flinging open the door to her room and shining a flashlight in my eyes, demanding to know why I'm walking around in the middle of the night. Because she definitely would do something like that.

Safely back in my room, I read over the form. Doesn't seem too complicated. It's only one page. Just a few blanks to fill in about your proposed invention. The form's the easy part, but can I actually do this? Sure, I have an idea, and it sounds good right now, but making it a reality is a whole 'nother thing.

What did Gilardi say? Science is life and life is science and all that. And how I should sleep on it, and "work within the system." What does that even mean?

I open my laptop and type that into the search bar. After finding lots of things that don't explain it at all and don't even make sense (because that's the Internet), I stumble on this: To really change something, you must change the rules. Work within the system, not against it.

Wait. What? Change the rules? Was Gilardi secretly telling me to work within the system to change McNutt rule number seven? Maybe she gets it and agrees kids shouldn't have to sit at their desks all the time! Unlike Delman, she'd be the kind of teacher who would.

It's two thirty. I yawn, shut my laptop, and get back into bed.

I slide *The Carrot Seed* under my pillow and pull up the comforter. I close my eyes, get that heavy feeling right before you fall asleep. And then I'm not in my bed, in my room, in my house. I'm standing at the top of the jungle gym, ready to jump.

I can feel the cool air on my face and see the tips of my gym shoes balanced on the edge and hear the shouts of the kids on the playground. My hands are wrapped tightly around the metal poles, but I'm so tall, my head hits the top and I have to crouch.

I'm twelve, not six.

And I'm standing there, hoping I remember how to fly.

CHAPTER THIRTEEN

Adaptation

BRIAN

On Thursday, Ethan tells me on the bus that he thinks we should do Invention Day.

I'm literally speechless for a few seconds. I was gonna tell him about seeing Jamie at Target and ask for his take on the situation, but then he comes up with this out of nowhere.

He waves his hand in front of my face. "Hello? Did you hear what I just said?"

"I don't even know how to respond. Except, are you really Ethan Marcus, or an alien nerd who took over his body last night while he slept?"

He laughs.

I shake my head. "Two days in Reflection, they completely brainwashed you. I can't believe it."

"No, really."

“No, really, what?”

“Kowalski, I have an idea.”

“You have an idea.”

“Yes! So, hey, you know that little kid book *The Carrot Seed*?”

“No. Never heard of it.”

“Okay, doesn’t matter. You and me, we’re gonna make something for Invention Day.”

I practically choke on my own saliva. “Invention Day. You and me? Brian Kowalski and Ethan Marcus.”

“Yeah.”

“What are we making?”

“The desk-evator.”

“Okay, sure. What the heck is that?”

“I thought of the idea last night. It’s an invention that kids can put on their desks to raise up their desktop so they can stand instead of sit all day. Desk-evator, you know, like elevator.”

“Piece of cake. When do we start?”

Ethan elbows me. “I’m not joking.”

“I know you’re not joking, and it’s scaring me. You and me, making this desk-evator thing? You realize that

I'm better at breaking things than making them? This morning, I somehow broke off the refrigerator handle. My mom had to tape it back on."

"We can do this! How hard could it be?"

I groan. "Hard."

"Listen. When they see how much better it is for kids not to be chained to their desks all day, they'll change rule number seven."

"Rule number seven?"

"Sit at your own desk. Feet and chair legs on the floor at all times."

"There's a good reason they have that rule. When my brother was at McNutt, some kid tipped back in his chair and cracked his head open."

"That did not happen."

"Okay, but he got a concussion, apparently. Anyway, dude, I know you have an issue with sitting. Your scoma thing. I get it. But Invention Day isn't the answer. I'm not doing it."

"You have to. I need you."

"Ethan, this is gonna require *tools*. Hammers and nails and stuff. And diagrams, models, probably even the use of geometry. And, like . . . engineering! We'd be a complete train wreck."

"No, we won't."

"What teacher at McNutt would let a kid have a desk-evator on their desk anyway?"

He grins, wiggles his eyebrows. "You never know. This is something called working within the system. Getting the rules to change."

I roll my eyes. "Oh, okay, sure. That makes perfect sense. Are you positive you didn't fall out of bed and hit your head on something?"

"No. Hey, what'd you say about your mom? How her standing desk is saving her life? People at work are able to stand. Why not at school?"

"Because. It's *school*."

He looks around the bus, then leans toward me. "Jamie Pappas will think you're really smart. Apparently, she told Parneeta she likes smart guys."

"Seriously?"

"Uh-huh."

"Because if that's not true, you're playing really dirty."

"I swear, it's true."

"Does she also like short guys?"

"That, I don't know."

I think about it for approximately one second. "Okay, I changed my mind. I'm in."

We slap hands.

The bus pulls up at McNutt and I grab my backpack. "You realize that besides making the desk-evator, which I don't even know how that's going to happen, you have to do a trifold display board. Total nightmare. The glue alone can kill you."

"I got it covered."

"You do?"

"Yeah."

Everyone stands and starts getting off the bus. I move to the aisle and wait for the kids in front of me to go. I always see her on the way to my locker, and when I get inside, there she is.

Jamieeee.

I know I'm obsessed. Don't get on me about it. I can be obsessed if I want to.

ETHAN

I filled out the form this morning while I was eating my cereal. Erin was thankfully in the bathroom, "getting ready" for school. It takes her an hour to do what up there, I don't know. I pretty much brush my teeth and I'm done.

Anyway, the form. I had to answer some questions and explain what my proposed invention would be. Wasn't too hard, like I thought. What, you don't believe me? You want to see it? Okay, sure. Here it is:

> HAVE YOU ALWAYS DREAMED OF BECOMING A YOUNG INVENTOR? HAVE YOU FOUND AN INTERESTING PROBLEM AND THOUGHT OF A WAY TO SOLVE IT?
>
> Calling all ideas! We invite you to participate in McNutt Junior High's second Invention Day, to be held November 9 at 7 p.m. in the gym. Make your invention, along with a trifold display board explaining the problem and how your invention will solve it, and you could earn a chance to receive an actual US patent.

Please work on your own or with one and only one partner. Entrants will be judged in three categories: functionality, creativity, and marketability. To enter, please fill out this form and return it to Ms. Gilardi, eighth-grade science, room 9.

1. Names and grade(s): Ethan Marcus, seventh grade, and Brian Kowalski, seventh grade.

2. Explain the problem you plan to tackle: How kids sit all day in school and get fidgety and can't concentrate and their brains turn to soup.

3. Describe your proposed invention: The desk-evator. It will be this thing you can put on your desk to raise up the desktop so you can stand if you need to.

4. Briefly explain how your invention will work: It will have a base, two sides that move up and down, and a top. It will clip onto the desk.

5. Illustrate how this could be marketed:

You know how when you go to a football game, you can rent a cushy seat and it clamps on the bleachers? Classrooms could have desk-evators available to fidgety kids who need them when they've had enough sitting. They could be in every school, basically, everywhere.

That's it. Not bad, huh?

Once I'm off the bus and inside, I quickly walk to Gilardi's room so I can turn in the form before the bell rings. And before my sister finds out and laughs hysterically in my face again.

When I get there, Wesley's sitting on the side counter, and it looks like he and Gilardi are hanging out or something.

Gilardi waves. "Ethan, come in."

"Yeah, uh, hi."

Wesley eyes me, kicks his boots against the cabinet.

"What can I do for you?" Gilardi asks.

"So, I thought about it, and I decided to do Invention Day."

She clasps her hands. "Wonderful! I'm thrilled to hear that!"

I give her my form as Wesley pushes himself off the counter and saunters over.

Gilardi reads what I've written. "Quite an interesting idea. I've never seen this one before. Okay, you're working with Brian Kowalski?"

"Yeah."

"Great. I'm so glad. You won't regret it. You'll never forget this experience, I'll tell you that much." She pushes up her pink glasses. "What changed your mind, Ethan?"

I kind of laugh. "Well, my spontaneous standing protest got me nowhere. So, I guess it was what you said about working within the system to change the rules."

I don't really want to bring up *The Carrot Seed*, even though that's part of it. I probably wouldn't have anyway, but with Wesley there, for sure I'm not going into that. I don't even want to imagine what he'd do if he found out I have a soft spot for a little kid book.

Gilardi nods. "Good choice. Let me know if you run into any roadblocks. My door's always open."

"Thanks. I will." I walk out, then go up the stairs to math.

To be honest, I told Brian I did, but I don't have this whole thing figured out. Does anyone who invents something? Do they know exactly what they're doing at first or do they just have an idea?

Last night I read online that Thomas Edison, the light bulb guy, had thousands of fails before he got it right. Thousands! I can't even believe he kept on trying after, like, five hundred. And the Wright Brothers crashed a bunch of planes before they got one to work.

I know one thing for sure right now, and that's okay: where to start.

This weekend me and Brian are gonna plant a carrot seed.

WESLEY

"Loser," I mutter.

"I don't think so," Gilardi says. "He's giving it a try. Nothing loser-ish about that."

"Whatever. Back to the seagulls. I still don't get why

they're living in the park. They're, like, homeless. Don't they need the ocean? How do they have enough water?"

"Actually, large populations of seagulls now live on land. It's a great example of adaptation, Wesley. They've become urban birds. There's ample food to be found in garbage cans, plenty of man-made ponds, as well as protection from their predators."

"People hate them."

"I wouldn't say that. They're quite aggressive, but very smart."

"They're loud and hostile and cause trouble."

Gilardi lowers her glasses, studies me. She knows what I'm getting at. "Perhaps," she says. "But they serve a purpose, like anything else. They're important."

"Important? Some lost seagulls?"

"Of course."

Her students start coming in.

"See you after school?" she asks. "We'll continue this interesting discussion?"

I shrug to make it look like I don't care.

I leave the room and walk toward the gym. I have PE first. Kearney, the gym teacher, is as disappointed in me as Dad, I think. Kearney knows I quit wrestling. He's always spewing crap like *You're not finished when you lose. You're finished when you quit.* And *Winners train, losers complain.*

Yeah, right.

I'm by the locker-room door when one of the wrestling guys shoves past me, then lets the door slam in my face. Thanks, man.

Then I see Marcus in the hallway. Even if I wanted to try and say something to a kid like him—*hey* or *how's it goin'*—it would come out stupid-sounding. He's with his friend anyway.

So I don't say anything and I go into the locker room and pull off my boots and change for gym and just deal with it.

Nothin' else I can do.

CHAPTER FOURTEEN

The Basement

ERIN

Something is going on with my brother.

At nine a.m. Saturday morning, Ethan's awake and in the kitchen, wearing what he calls "school clothes," which are jeans and a T-shirt that isn't ripped. Usually, he doesn't come downstairs until almost lunch, and every weekend, no matter if it's August or January, he wears long shorts and these old, faded sleeveless shirts with—can I just mention this gross fact—his underarm hair poking out.

Ew, right? I know.

Anyway, I ask him what he's doing up so early, but he shrugs and gets the cereal and milk, like this isn't anything out of the ordinary. Then he stands at the counter eating his cereal, crunching and slurping milk from the bowl.

A half hour later, Brian Kowalski rings the doorbell and comes inside. Ethan takes the glue from the kitchen drawer and gets his laptop. Brian's carrying a big plastic bag with who knows what inside, and a TRIFOLD DISPLAY BOARD. That's when I knew for sure something was going on. The two of them with a trifold display board? It's not safe.

They go down to the basement, shutting the door behind them. When Zoe arrives, she and I get to work in the garage on our research with the invasive plant species, but I'm having trouble concentrating. I keep wondering what they're doing in the basement. I mean, wouldn't you?

On top of it, when I go inside for a drink of water (and yes, to listen at the basement door), the printer in Dad's office is spitting out page after page. Mom and Dad aren't home, so I know it's the boys. What are they printing on a Saturday morning, when Ethan always leaves his homework until the last minute on Sunday night?

Finally I can't stand it any longer. I tell Zoe we should take a break and casually mention that my brother and Brian are in the basement. "Let's go say hi, okay?"

Her cheeks get bright pink, and then she starts giggling, which turns into nervous-sounding hiccups. "I didn't even know—*hiccup*—your brother—*hiccup*—was home."

I tilt my head. "Are you okay?"

"Fine!" she squeaks.

We go inside the house, and I softly open the basement door, then tiptoe down the stairs with Zoe right behind me.

Our basement, by the way, is creepy and chilly and full of spiders. It's unfinished, so there are all sorts of metal pipes and wood beams on the ceiling, plus a cement floor and walls, an infinite amount of spooky-looking cobwebs, and bare light bulbs. The only furniture is an old, lumpy sofa, a TV, and Dad's broken air hockey table from when he was a kid.

Ethan, for some reason, loves the basement. I do not. I barely ever go down there, but today, an exception must be made.

When I peek around the bottom of the stairs, I see Ethan lying on his stomach on the icky floor, looking at his laptop screen, and Brian gluing a piece of paper to the trifold display board, which is propped on the sofa. Their backs are to us.

"Hey, guys," I announce, and both of them jump.

Ethan quickly closes his laptop and bolts up. "What are you doing, Erin? Spying on us?"

"No, we just came down to say hi."

"Hi, Ethan." Zoe waves, giggling and hiccuping again.

"Hi." He glares at me. "Okay, you've said hi. Now if you don't mind."

Brian folds the display board, then stands in front of it and crosses his arms, like he's guarding it.

I try to look past Brian. "What's the big secret?"

"It's none of your business. Just go back upstairs!" Ethan shouts.

"You guys aren't . . ." I look back and forth from Ethan to Brian. "Don't tell me . . ."

Zoe claps. "Wait! Are you guys doing Invention Day? Something related to your protest, Ethan? That's *so* cool!"

"Seriously?" I raise an eyebrow and give him a look. (Mom's training me; I've almost got it down.)

"Fine," my brother says. "If you want to know so badly, we are, okay?"

"Hold on. Do you know what you're getting into here?"

Brian rolls his eyes. "Go ahead, Erin McBarren, tell us we're idiots and we're out of our league and we're gonna fail."

Zoe shakes her head, her long ponytail swinging from side to side. "She wouldn't do that!"

Brian smirks. "Yes, she would. In a second."

"I won't, I promise. So what's your invention? Maybe we can help. Give you some advice."

Ethan kicks a pen that's on the floor and it rolls into a corner. "We don't need any advice."

"It's something about the problem of sitting too much in school, right?" Zoe asks. "Sorry, I saw the board before you closed it."

I nod. Now it's making sense. "Oh, I get it. You want to invent something to solve your ESD issue?"

Zoe looks confused. "What's ESD?"

"Nothing," Ethan snaps.

I walk to the display board. "Can I see?"

Brian's holding the glue bottle out in front of him with two hands, like he might squirt it in my face or use it as a weapon.

"I come in peace," I say.

"Whatever," Ethan mutters. "She's not going to give up. Like a barracuda. Just let her look at it."

Brian gives me a little sneer, then lowers the glue bottle and steps aside.

When I unfold the board, I see they've glued on a few sheets of paper. One says: SITTING IS THE NEW SMOKING, and another says: CONSTANT SITTING PUTS YOU AT RISK OF MANY DISEASES.

"Hmm. Not bad. I have to admit, I'm actually kind of impressed. But what's your invention?"

They don't say anything.

I turn and look at them, then do another eyebrow raise, for effect. "You do realize you need an actual invention? Not just all these facts about the problem, right?"

"How clueless do you think we are?" Brian huffs. "We have one. And it's good. Real good. But that, we're not telling you."

"Yeah," Ethan adds. "Now can you get out of here, please?"

I point to the plastic bag that Brian brought. It's on

the floor by the sofa, but it's twist-tied so I can't see what's inside. "Those are your supplies?"

Ethan stamps his foot. "Erin! Leave!"

"Fine! Be that way!" I grab Zoe's arm and pull her toward the stairs.

Zoe smiles at Ethan. "Maybe we can all break for lunch together. I brought some homemade granola."

He shrugs. "I don't know, maybe."

I start to go up. "Well, we've got *loads* of work to do with invasive plants. To basically save every forest in the country. Not to mention life as we know it."

Zoe waves. "Bye, Ethan." She skips up the stairs.

"We'll be in the garage if you change your mind," I call.

Ethan zooms up behind me and practically pushes us out. "We won't." He slams the basement door.

ETHAN

When I come back down, Brian says, "Well, that was pleasant. Always fun to hang with your sister."

"Really. She's getting more annoying, if that's even possible." I open my laptop. "So, where were we?"

"You were on the site with that doctor dude who thinks people weren't meant to sit all day and chairs are slowly killing us."

"Right. You know, he says that standing for three or four hours a day is equal to running ten marathons a year?"

"That's crazy. Man, I think I sit for like, I don't know . . ." Brian counts on his fingers. He sucks at math. "Whoa, it's close to twelve hours! Half the freakin' day!"

"I know. And most of that's in school."

I go back to the site and print more stuff for the display board. I practically never want to sit in a chair again. You can get fat, weaken your muscles, mess up your spine. Then there's this little-known scary fact: you use more energy chewing gum than you do slouching in a chair.

And my personal favorite—photos of two brain scans, one of a "sitting" brain and the other of a "moving" brain. The sitting one looks like the person could be dead. The moving one is lit up like a fireworks show.

You tell me how a kid with the sitting brain is supposed to focus and concentrate in school. Impossible, right? See, scomas are a real thing. I knew it.

Then I somehow come across a quote from Charles Dickens. He used a standing desk, and so did Thomas Jefferson and Ernest Hemingway! Whoa. I love those guys. They got it.

I shout to Brian, who's got glue all over his fingers and is trying to unstick them. "C'mere! Look at this!"

He reads over my shoulder. "That's awesome. Wait, Dickens? Wasn't he in that movie we saw with the giant aliens?"

"No! He wrote famous books, like . . ." I can't even think of one.

"Oh, yeah, that guy. *A Tale of Two Cities*, right? My brother's reading it for freshman English."

"Yes! Who would argue with anything Charles Dickens said?"

I type the quote, hit the print button, then run upstairs to grab it from Dad's office. I come back down and hand it to Brian to glue onto the board.

> "If I could not walk far and fast, I think I should just explode and perish."
>
> —Charles Dickens

"The explode part is great," I say. "Because that's how I feel in class every day."

Brian makes an explosion sound, then falls to the floor.

"Exactly."

We've explained the problem we plan to tackle. Now, step two: inventing the desk-evator.

We can do this. WE can do this!

Right?

ZOE

Increased energy? Check.

Racing heartbeat? Check.

Loss of appetite? Breathless? Can't stop thinking about him? Check, check, check.

The quiz on my phone gives me my score: twenty-five points. I gasp. Then this flashes on the screen, with little pulsing red hearts: NO DOUBT ABOUT IT, GIRL. YOU ARE IN LOVE!

"Zoe!" Erin snaps her fingers. "Are you doing this with me or not?"

"Sorry, I just got a little distracted by something." I slide the phone into my back pocket.

"I'll say. Come on, we were going to test the garlic next."

"Right, right."

Erin picks up a little bottle, then jots something on a pad of paper. "Okay, trial number one with garlic."

I walk over and stand next to her, but I feel kind of dizzy. Don't be alarmed, I'm still very concerned about the invasive plant problem. But all I can think at the moment is . . . Zoe Feld-Kramer, welcome to a whole new world!

It's confirmed.

There's no denying it anymore: you are in love with Ethan Marcus!

CHAPTER FIFTEEN

Step Two

ETHAN

Brian and I hang out in the basement all day, but somehow we never get around to the desk-evator. We watch a movie, make up this basketball game where the ball has to land on the air hockey table, then basically spend the rest of the time eating bags of pretzels, popcorn, Chex Mix; whatever we can find in the pantry.

Then, around five, we decide that we should have a sleepover so we can work on our invention on Sunday. Mom says it's okay with her if it's okay with Brian's mom, which it is. We ask if we can sleep in the basement, but she says no right off the bat. She wrinkles her nose, shakes her head, even sticks out her tongue.

"You know I like to let you make your own decisions, but it's disgusting down there," she says.

It really isn't. I don't know why Mom and Erin think

that. (1) It's cooler than any other room in my house (I'm talking temperature), so when I'm sweaty from shooting baskets outside or it's a boiling summer day, the basement is by far the best place to be, (2) it's completely private, and (3) when Erin's freaking out about something, it's a good spot to hide out in until she calms down.

The greatest part is that the spiderwebs and light bulbs make it feel like a cave, plus there's a decent echo if you stand in the corner and yell, which I used to do all the time when I was little.

There was one time Erin wanted to use the basement. She's probably still mad about what happened. Brian and I had set up this obstacle course where you had to jump over blobs of bubble gum. After we were done, we kind of forgot about it. How was I supposed to know that Erin was having a slumber party the next day and the girls were gonna pretend to pan for gold in the basement?

I thought it was funny—everyone had gum on their feet and one girl had a glop in her hair—but Erin said I messed everything up, "like usual."

Anyway.

Mom says she doesn't understand why Brian and I

can't sleep in my room, and I'm trying to come up with reasons, but then Dad just goes, "Let 'em stay in the basement. What's the difference?"

Finally Mom says all right. She must've realized this is her chance to clean out my room. I bet a bag of my old T-shirts will be at Goodwill before I figure out what's missing.

We order a pizza. Dad comes down and tries to fix the air hockey game, because he really wants us to play it. He tells Brian he was the air hockey champion of his neighborhood when he was our age. I already knew that. Anyway, after a half hour, he bangs the table with a fist, unplugs it, and gives up.

"It's okay, Dad," I say. "We'll survive without air hockey."

He flicks the puck with a finger, but it barely moves. "It's just such a great game. You know I beat Joey Mancuso twelve times in a row one summer?"

Brian and I don't say anything. I don't want to break it to Dad that nobody plays air hockey anymore.

He sighs, walks to the stairs. "Not too late, guys."

After we hear the basement door close, we start

talking about all kinds of stuff; the kind of stuff you think isn't important, but really is.

Like how come some people think pencils are a perfectly fine thing to give out at Halloween. And why Señora Pling has a fit whenever we can't remember a Spanish word for something. Which Hogwarts house we'd be in. How my neighbors have this miniature tree in the shape of a Hershey's kiss. And what's up with Wesley Pinto.

"Personally," Brian says, "I think the dude is all show and no action."

"Possible. It's a good show, though. I definitely don't want to mess with him."

"Yeah, really. Maybe he was bullied or something when he was little, so he wants to act like he's so tough."

"It's weird, though. When I went to Gilardi's room to turn in the form, he was there. It seemed like he was, I don't know, hanging out."

"Very weird."

We move on to Jamie and how she talked to Brian in Target and if that means she likes him. Then we start imitating our teachers' voices and cracking up over their first names. Mr. Kearney, the gym teacher, is Kirby,

Señora Pling is Florentina, and Mr. Delman is Grover! Who names their kid Grover? Didn't his parents realize that's a character on *Sesame Street*?

I don't know what time we end up falling asleep, but it must be late, because the next morning, we don't wake up until after eleven. We toast bagels for breakfast, then hurry back to the basement to start working on the desk-evator.

Brian dumps out all these things from the plastic bag—a couple of Slinkys, pieces of cardboard, the lid from a plastic box, a screwdriver, a handle from something, giant rubber bands, and some kind of metal tripod stand. And a stack of stuck-together square-shaped red and green magnets.

I look over the pile. Unlike my mom, Brian's mom doesn't throw anything away. "Magnets? What are those for?"

"I don't know." He shrugs. "I was just grabbing anything. Found 'em under my bed. Could be useful."

"Okay. So . . . any thoughts here with this stuff?"

He jabs me. "I got some thoughts."

"Go for it."

He takes one piece of cardboard, puts the Slinkys on opposite ends, then lays another piece of cardboard on top of them. "So what if the Slinkys expand and push up the top cardboard when you want to stand at your desk. It wouldn't really be cardboard. Or Slinkys. This is just to demonstrate how it could work. The concept, you know?"

"Gotcha."

Brian tries it, and the Slinkys fall as soon as he lets go. "I mean, we'd have to figure out how it would stay up, I guess. And what we'd really use."

I grin. "And who said you can't make things?"

"Funny. Your turn."

I pace around the basement, jumping and trying to touch the metal pipes on the ceiling. "So basically, we need a base, two movable sides, and a top. And some way for it to clip onto the desk."

"Sounds good to me."

"But what do we use to make that?"

"Not Slinkys."

I crouch, pick up the tripod. "What was this from?"

"The bottom of an old music stand we had. I don't even know why we had it, because no one in my family ever played an instrument. My mom, she just buys things for no reason."

"Yeah. Could be an idea for the base, though?"

"Maybe."

We get to work, trying to make a desk-evator from the stuff Brian brought and other junk I find in the crawl space that seem like legit hardware-type items. Shelf brackets, hinges, a couple of metal rods. We even play around with the magnets for a while, but we end up making designs that look more like miniature tables and unstable bridges, not a model for a desk-evator.

After a couple of hours, Brian smacks his forehead with his hand. "YouTube."

I groan. "Why didn't we think of that before?"

I run upstairs. Erin's in the family room. As I pass her, she says, "How's it going?" but I don't answer. I grab my laptop charger (battery at 8 percent) and rush back down. I search "standing desks," then find a video with this guy in a dorky plaid short-sleeved shirt who's showing how to make your own standing desk.

"Excellent," I say, pushing play. "This'll definitely help."

The guy lays out some tools and materials, explains

how easy it is, and says no one should pay for the expensive standing desks you can buy.

A few minutes in, Brian taps my shoulder. "Uh . . . he's using a power sander. Do you know how to use a power sander?"

"No."

"And a power screwdriver."

"I see."

"This is *easy*?" Brian snorts. "For him. Maybe he works in construction or something?"

"Agree. This is way too complicated."

We watch another video about how an elevator works, because that's what we want the idea to be, but that's complicated too. Steel cables, an electric motor, hydraulic fluid, centrifugal force.

Brian stretches out on his back, clasps his hands behind his head. "If we need to know about centrifugal force, I might be out, Marcus."

"It can't be this hard." I keep searching YouTube for something that'll help. I find a few more videos, but nothing all that useful.

Dad comes down to see if he can give us an assist,

but then he studies our mess and strokes his beard, which he does when (1) he's trying to figure out a problem, or (2) can't figure out a problem. "Sorry, guys," he says, "this is way above me. I'm a lowly accountant, not a structural engineer."

Mom manages an eye doctor's office, so I doubt she could give us any help either. Unless one of us needs glasses.

Brian's breathing heavy and his eyes are closed. While he zones out, I work on the desk-evator design some more. I end up with this shaky, wobbly thing made out of the metal rods, hinges, and the plastic lid. I have no idea what to use for the base or how it would clip onto a desk at school.

Brian opens his eyes and sits up just as the thing I made collapses.

"Okay, so it needs some work," I say.

He nods. "Maybe a little."

Let me tell you, the carrot seed approach, it isn't as straightforward as it looks on the page.

CHAPTER SIXTEEN

Seagulls

WESLEY

Mom calls from Florida on Sunday night, but when Dad hands me the phone, I tell him I don't want to talk. He doesn't push it. What's she gonna say anyway? *How's school* and *How're you doing* and *I miss you*?

Yeah, if you missed me, you wouldn't be in the Sunshine State, would you?

My parents split last year, which was better than them yelling at each other all the time. So that's an improvement. But then Mom decided she wanted to "find herself" in Florida. What the heck does that mean?

Brett and me are supposed to go there and live with her when she gets a big enough place and a job and gets "settled." She told Dad she's living with a friend at the moment. I think it's this guy she dated before she and Dad got married. Don't ask me why I think that, I just do. Okay, I saw his name come up on her phone a few times. Barry. What a stupid name.

Neither of us wants to go. Brett's got wrestling, and I've got, I don't know, but I don't think it'll be any better in Florida. The people there will be the same as the people at McNutt, only more tan. Everyone's got their group.

I'm brushing my teeth when Brett barges into the bathroom and throws his arms around my neck in a choke hold. It's a takedown in two seconds, because I don't even try anymore.

"You suck, man!" he shouts. "This used to be fun, you and me messing around!"

I stand and spit toothpaste at him. "It was never fun." I rinse my mouth and go into my room, slamming the door.

Sometimes I get so mad about everything—Mom leaving, Dad trying but coming off helpless and sad, Brett pounding me and thinking it's brother stuff, plus every day in school being boring and pointless. I don't even know what to do. I feel like those seagulls in the park, lost and living somewhere I don't belong.

I grab my pillow, then throw it across the room. It lands in a corner and a few feathers fly out. I watch them float to the floor.

Gilardi has a blue knitted pillow on her chair. She made it, I think. Once, when I was mad about something—can't even remember what—she told me to punch it. I didn't. I thought that sounded dumb.

But now, I pick up my pillow and ram my fist into it a couple of times. It does feel dumb. But also, good.

The talks with Gilardi started when I was the only one in there for Reflection and she'd ask me what I thought about stuff. At first I didn't even bother to answer, because I figured she was like every other teacher I'd had. They act like they care but they really don't. They have their own crap going on. Their own lives. Everyone does.

One day I answered her. I don't even remember why I did, or what the question was. But we ended up talking about whether homework is good practice or just busywork, and unless she was great at faking it, she seemed interested in what I had to say. I was kinda floored. No teacher ever did something like that. Listened. Really listened.

Then we started talking about other stuff. All kinds of stuff.

Now I go to her room in the mornings, or after school if I want. I only talk when no one else is there. People don't need to hear what's going on in my head. I don't even want to hear what's going on in my head half the time.

Yeah, when I wrestled, I was friends with those guys. We sorta talked, I guess. I was in their group. They think I quit because I kept losing matches. No. I quit because I hated it and was sick of what you have to do to make weight. They kept at it and I didn't. Nothing in common anymore.

Dad knocks on my door and comes in. "You okay, Wes?"

"Never better."

He stands in the doorway. He looks thinner. "Want to chat?"

"Why? What's it gonna do? How's it gonna help?"

"Look, I know it's been hard on you, but eventually, you're going to have to accept—"

"I don't have to do anything." I get up and close the door.

I know he stands there for a few seconds, on the other side. I can hear him breathing. I almost open the door, but then it gets quiet.

You know what my wrestling coach said my problem was? That my opponent could sense my weakness as soon as we stepped onto the mat. That he knew he could beat me before the match even started.

And you know what else?

I think that's true.

CHAPTER SEVENTEEN

Romanov

ETHAN

Monday, Brian and I are at lunch. Everyone sits at long tables with benches. It's another rule. More square butt happening here.

The cafeteria monitors walk around and blow their whistles at people for who knows what. They're 100 percent serious about order in the cafeteria. They also have walkie-talkies to use when necessary.

Erin and Zoe and their girl group are by the salad bar, giggling and talking in screechy high voices, like a table of monkeys. There are your usual other tables—the athletes, the mathletes, the theater people, the computer guys, the popular kids. You can get up to buy a drink or a hot lunch or throw your garbage away, but that's about it. No goofing around, no throwing food, and we'll all get along just fine.

Brian's sitting across from me. I lean toward him. "Okay, I thought about this all last night. You know what we need?"

He's lining up the contents of his lunch—yogurt, cheese, a hard-boiled egg, milk, a piece of chicken. "No, tell me, what do we need?"

I look at everything on the table. "Wait, why do you have all this?"

He peels open the yogurt. "My new plan. It's all protein, to make me grow. Tomorrow I'm gonna be taller than you."

"Got it. Okay, good luck with that. Anyway, as I was gonna say, I think we need assistance."

Brian opens his milk carton and slurps it. "Agree. I'm thinkin' we're more like the idea guys."

"Exactly. We need someone who can help us make the desk-evator. Did Mark Zuckerberg design Facebook alone? No, he thought of the idea, then got genius-type people to help him make it happen."

Brian nods, keeps eating.

"I mean, the whole point is to show people how great standing desks would be in school, but we can't screw up the invention with some embarrassing piece of junk that doesn't even work."

"Right."

I slap my hand on the table and the spoon falls out of Brian's yogurt. "So what we have to do is to rent a genius."

He picks up the spoon and licks it. "Too bad there's not an app for that. Maybe we should contact Zuckerberg."

"We don't have to. Romanov is right here."

Brian's mouth drops open and some yogurt dribbles onto his chin. "Romanov."

"Yeah."

"Are you nuts? One, he's already doing his own project, and two, why would he help us?"

I shrug. "Maybe he hates sitting too. Did you ever think of that?"

"No. Things like that don't bother Romanov. He's a machine."

We look over to the table by the vending area where Romanov sits. He's on one end, and this kid with big hair is at the other end. That's it, no one else. Romanov has what looks like a package of sushi in front of him, and a black water bottle to match his black skinny jeans. He's reading. I can't tell what, but it's a book with about four million times more pages than *The Carrot Seed.* After a few minutes of watching the guy, I can tell you he hasn't raised his eyes from the book once. Excellent focus. Just what we need.

Brian shakes his head. "I don't know. If I was Romanov, and I'm glad I'm not because I would be scared of myself, why would I bother to help two guys like us?"

"Because maybe we'll be the first people in school history who talk to him?"

"He doesn't care about that, obviously."

"Everyone cares about that. Anyway, the thing is"—I lower my voice—"after yesterday, I'm not sure we can make the desk-evator without a brain like him."

"Good point."

I get up, and Mrs. Hinkley, one of the monitors, eyes me. "I'm just going to talk to someone," I say.

Hinkley brushes her hand like, be quick about it.

I start walking toward Romanov. The guy doesn't glance up once, not when it's pretty clear I'm heading his way, and not when I sit down across from him.

"Hi," I say.

He doesn't look at me.

"How ya doin'?"

He flicks his eyes from the book like I'm barely worth his time. His eyes are dark brown, almost black. I can't even see the pupils.

"I'm Ethan Marcus," I start, and then he goes (still not looking at me), "I know who you are."

Not like that's creepy or anything.

"Well, so I was wondering if you might give me and my friend Brian Kowalski a hand with our Invention Day project. We're trying to make something so kids can stand at their desks—"

He carefully folds over the corner of the page he's reading, then closes the book and sets it down. "I do my own projects."

"I know that, but we just need some advice, a little guidance, maybe. You can still do your own project. I'm not asking you to—"

He shakes his head, but not in a normal way. Just one slight motion to the right and an even slighter one to the left. "I don't give advice."

"Okay, not advice. We just have a few questions, and I thought—"

His shoulders drop and he does this long sigh, like I'm annoying him and he wishes I would leave. "If you can't do your project, you should not be doing Invention Day. There is no room for people who are not serious."

Whoa. Okay. I go for the Hail Mary. "You could, like, hang out with me and Brian. I have a really cool basement—"

"No." He picks up the book. It's Shakespeare; an old, thick, worn-out gigantic book that looks like it's actually from when Shakespeare lived. I guess that means this conversation is over?

I stand. "Nice talking to you, Marlon."

I hurry toward my table before Hinkley can nail me. Then I see my sister—and a few other kids, including Wesley—staring at me. Erin's shaking her head the Erin way—disgusted, aggravated, mad.

"How could you?" she mouths.

I shrug like I don't know what she means, and then she whips around so her back is to me.

When I reach my table, Brian goes, “Went well?”

I nod. “Very.”

“Back to you and me, engineer brains that we are?”

I grit my teeth. “We’re gonna do this. Somehow. We’re going to make a desk-evator. I promise you.”

He fake-coughs. “Like you promised I wouldn’t get sick on that upside-down roller coaster?”

“This,” I say, “is different. I don’t want to win, I want to change the rules. For me, for you, for kids in school everywhere.” I make a fist. “Our time has come. Scoma time.”

Brian claps. “Nice speech.”

“Are you with me?”

He glances in Jamie’s direction. “Sure.”

I plunk onto the bench. “Thanks.”

“Ah, forget about Romanov,” Brian says. “He’s weird and we don’t need him.”

“You bet we don’t. We got this.”

CHAPTER EIGHTEEN

A Big Deal

ERIN

What in the world was my brother doing? I know he has a thing about me getting better grades, and generally being an all-around more together person (never late with assignments, never lose homework, always working ahead), but I never dreamed he would go this far. Talking to the enemy? If Ethan told Marlon *anything* about my Invention Day project, this would absolutely be the worst thing he's ever done to me.

When I get home after school, he's not there. Of course, he's walking. I pace around the kitchen, eating an apple, rehearsing what I plan to say the minute he comes in the door. He strolls in around four thirty with his jacket unzipped and his shoes untied. I pounce. "Ethan! What were you doing at lunch talking to Marlon Romanov?"

He gives me that chill, unworried look of his. "Calm down."

"Don't say that. I am not calming down. Please explain!"

He opens the fridge and takes out something wrapped in foil. "Is this the pizza from last week?"

I stamp my foot. "I don't know!"

He unwraps the foil; it is the pizza, and he takes a huge bite. "Stop freaking out, Erin. I just thought Romanov could give us an assist. We're having some issues with our project, and I asked if he could help us."

"But . . . I offered to help you."

Ethan shrugs, eats more of the pizza.

"Besides, you know that's against the rules. You and Brian signed up together; you can't work with another person. And why would you go to *him*, of all people? You know Marlon's my archenemy."

Ethan rolls his eyes. "Your archenemy? Isn't that a bit dramatic?"

"No, not at all. So that's it? You didn't tell him anything about what Zoe and I are doing?"

"I didn't, I swear. You actually think I'd do that?"

"I wasn't sure what was going on!"

"Well, don't worry, he blew me off. Barely said a word."

"Really?"

"Yes." He opens the fridge again, then closes it. "Can I ask you something? Why are you always so mad at me?"

"Not always. Just, a lot. And it's . . . well, if I had to sum it up, it's because of how you are."

"How I am. What are you talking about?"

"Don't act like you don't know what I mean. You do stuff, and things happen, or don't happen, and you're all like, no big deal, no worries, and you charm everyone, it always somehow works out, and Mom and Dad end up thinking you're the best son ever."

"Okay, that makes sense."

"Come on. Like when you broke that vase after Mom told you over and over not to play volleyball in the house. You ignore her, shatter the vase, then put a twenty-dollar bill on her desk and get a tear in your eye and tell her how sorry you are. And she's all like, 'Thank you for being honest and owning up to your mistake.'"

“Why would you be mad at that? It had nothing to do with you.”

I shake my head. “Then there was that time at Mom’s friend’s outdoor wedding.”

“What?”

“The puppy, the pond?”

“Oh yeah.” He starts laughing. “It was drowning.”

“It was not drowning. Dogs can swim, and you did not have to jump into the pond in your suit to rescue it. You’d think everyone would’ve been mad, but somehow they found it hilarious. Someone posted a video, remember? It got hundreds of likes.”

He grins. “What can I say?”

“The worst, though, is when we stayed in that hotel and you were obsessed with the waffle machine.”

“Yeah. Good times.”

“WAFFLES!” I shout. “You were so busy making waffles for everyone in the breakfast area, and then Dad joined in and he lost track of the time, and do you remember how we ended up missing our flight?”

Ethan groans. “That happened, like, two years ago. You’re still mad about it?”

"It's just, everything! And now, you go ask Marlon for help, not even thinking how it'll make me feel?"

"You'd be mad no matter what I did! And with the waffles, what was the big deal anyway? We got on the next flight, right? We got home."

I can't help it, I start to cry. "See, there you go. You're doing it right now—the 'What's the big deal?' thing. Did you ever stop to think that what's not a big deal to you might be a big deal to me?" I grab my backpack and start to leave the kitchen.

"Just say it, Erin. You hate me."

I stop, turn back, swallow hard. "It's more like grate."

"Great?"

"Grate on my nerves. Like fingernails on a chalkboard."

He nods. "I'm fingernails on a chalkboard. Thanks."

He goes down to the basement and I go upstairs to my room, then shut the door. I try not to give in to the crying because I don't like when that happens.

That day? The waffle/missed flight day? I'll tell you what happened. My best friend at the time—a girl I'd known since second grade—was moving away, and I told her I'd be back in time to say good-bye. When we finally got home, I ran the entire four blocks to her house. She was gone. No moving van, no cars. Nothing.

Her house was sad and lonely, and I couldn't even bear to look at it. We'd spent so much time there. We had so many inside jokes and memories.

I'd bought matching friendship bracelets on our trip, one for her and one for me, and I was so excited to give her the bracelet as a good-bye gift.

On the walk back to my house, I threw them both as far as I could. I didn't even watch where they landed. Hopefully in someone's trash.

I sobbed about it to Mom, and she said she felt terrible. But the thing was, it happened and it couldn't ever be fixed.

I didn't bother telling Ethan. He wouldn't have understood. And besides, even if I had, what difference would it make? He's the way he is and I'm the way I am and it's never going to change. We just don't get each other. Our brains don't work the same way.

I admit there've been times I secretly wished I was

an only child. I look at people who are close with their siblings and hang out with them all the time, like Zoe and her little sister, and Parneeta and her older brother. Then I'm not mad, just really, really sad. And I realize how much of a big deal it is, having a brother like Ethan.

CHAPTER NINETEEN

Glaring and Staring

ETHAN

Brian and I try more, and fail more. Whatever we make either falls apart or doesn't work. It's time to phone a friend.

I stop at Gilardi's room one morning and tell her I'm having trouble. She gives me a list of websites to check out and suggests I ask the librarian for some books on simple machines.

"Think pulleys," she says. "Or perhaps, levers. Then, if you're still stuck, what I like to do is get away from it for a while. I often find that the best ideas come when I'm not trying so hard." She holds up her knitting. "Some people walk, others do yoga. I knit."

"Thanks," I mutter, walking out. I kind of get what she's saying, but yoga? Knitting? Uh . . . I don't think so.

Brian and I find a bucket of Legos in my closet that

somehow escaped Goodwill, and we build a desk-evator model. We get really excited; then we look at it and go, okay, now what? How do we translate it to the real thing?

"Maybe we can use this?" Brian says.

"At Invention Day?" I ask. "No."

Brian's mom takes us to her office so we can see an actual standing desk. But the one she has isn't what I imagined. It's big and has a separate tray for her keyboard and looks even more complicated than the one the guy made on YouTube.

Dad even drives us to Home Depot so we can get better materials. The three of us wander the aisles and stare at shelves full of things like drywall compound and joist hangers.

Some bald guy in an orange apron seems to know what we need and directs us to the building material section, where we find supplies to build a house but not a desk-evator.

A different bald guy, also wearing an apron, approaches Brian. "Need some help, son?"

"Yeah," Brian cracks. "You know where I can buy one of those aprons? They're totally cool."

The guy says they're not for sale.

"Too bad. I really wanted one."

"You could apply for a job here," he says. "Are you sixteen?"

"I will be. In four years."

I pull Brian's sleeve and he waves to the guy. "Okay, bye! Nice talking to you. Let me know if the situation changes!"

After we drop off Brian at his house, Dad gives me a pep talk on the ride home. Stuff like, "When the going gets tough, the tough get going," and "Winners never quit and quitters never win."

"Dad," I say. "This isn't sports, and it's not about winning or quitting. There are two and a half weeks until Invention Day. At this point, it's about a miracle."

When I walk into the kitchen, Erin's sitting at the counter with her laptop. I open the fridge like I always do, hoping for something new and exciting, and then Erin says, "Mom, can you ask Ethan to close the refrigerator? It's blowing cold air on me."

I shake my head.

Erin's been speaking to me only through Mom or Dad. As in: "Mom, could you ask Ethan to pass the potatoes?"

And, "Dad, please remind Ethan that it's his turn to take out the garbage."

Even Mom and Dad are rolling their eyes at this. But they're sticking to their Parenting 101 philosophy and being very patient and calm, saying stuff like, "Erin, perhaps you could ask Ethan directly." She's not listening.

After I shut the refrigerator, Erin does this little huff, closes her laptop, then stands.

I spin around. "Is this all because I talked to Romanov? You're acting ridiculous."

She raises an eyebrow. "You still don't get it." She turns away, then looks back at me and lifts her chin. "And you know what? I didn't think you could do it."

"The desk-evator? You didn't think I could make the desk-evator? Is that what you're saying?"

"Oh, *that's* what you're calling your invention? Interesting name, at least. But you don't have what it takes."

I go back and forth between wanting to shout that she's wrong—she's never been more wrong in her life—to admitting she's right, but in the end, I just emit some sort of nonhuman sound.

We stand there glaring at each other for a few seconds.

Then, finally, I tear down to the basement and punch the trifold display board, still propped on the sofa. The middle section, where you're supposed to explain your invention and how it solves the problem, is blank. On the floor is the mess of random stuff we've been using to try to make the desk-evator. I kick the pile and everything scatters.

I don't know who I'm madder at right now: Erin . . . or myself.

She and I keep up the glaring and staring in the morning and on the bus. The whole day at school, I keep thinking the worst part of all is that I know in my heart this is a great idea. But what good is a great idea if you can't make it happen?

In LA that afternoon, Delman's explaining different types of reading strategies we need to "employ." His monotone voice is putting everyone in a trance. "Make connections. . . . Draw on background knowledge. . . . Interpret information from the text. . . ."

The room is boiling, and I'm way beyond ESD.

It's pretty much full-body paralysis at this point. *Petrificus Totalus.*

Erin's scribbling notes, but everyone else is barely awake. Zoe's eyelids are fluttering and her head is rolling from side to side. She was chewing gum, but now the wad is sort of suspended on her bottom lip. When her head drops forward, the gum falls out of her mouth and plops onto her desk. But she doesn't even wake up.

Suddenly Delman claps his hands several times and everyone jumps. "Pop quiz!" he says. "Right now!"

I force my eyelids open with my fingers, then reach into my backpack for a pencil. Grover Delman marches to his desk, picks up a stack of papers, then starts passing them out, facedown.

When everyone has one, he says, "You all should know this material by now. We've been going over it for days. I expect very few mistakes." He looks around the room. "You may begin."

I flip over my paper and read the first question. Out of the corner of my eye, I see Erin click her mechanical pencil to push up the lead, then hunch over her quiz. Her hand moves down the paper at lightning speed.

I shift in my chair, stretch my arms, crack my knuckles. Delman gives me a warning-type look. I answer question one, start number two. I'm on the third question when Erin puts her pencil down, turns her quiz over, and folds her hands on her desk. Her legs are crossed and she's sitting straight and still as a statue. I want to grab Zoe's gum and throw it at her.

Mean Secretary walks in and looks menacingly around the room at us. I'm surprised she was able to peel her butt from her chair. She hands Delman a folder, then walks out.

I go back to the quiz, but things are happening, you know? My legs are tingling, my brain is cloudy, and my hand is cramping. What I wouldn't give for a desk-evator right now. I could take the quiz while standing up and all would be good in the world.

Delman announces, "Three more minutes."

There's nothing else to do except randomly circle answers. I hear his loafer footsteps coming toward me. Soft little taps of doom.

"Finish up," he says, then stops next to my desk,

crosses his arms, and looks down at my quiz.

Teachers like to do that, the hovering thing, and today I'm the victim. The point on my pencil breaks and I can't even answer the last two questions.

"Okay," Delman says. "Time's up. Please pass your quizzes forward."

I give my quiz to the kid in front of me, then look at the clock. Still twenty minutes to go.

I'm gonna die in here one day.

CHAPTER TWENTY

Love and Grate

ZOE

On Saturday afternoon Erin and I are working in her garage on our experiments, but I'm finding it really hard to concentrate. Ethan (and Brian) are playing football on the grass. A few feet away!

Have you noticed the way his hair curls on the back of his neck? Or how his eyes crinkle into two lines when he laughs? It's so cute. And the way he goes, "Hi, Zoe." I could almost melt. What am I saying? I do melt!

Ethan calls, "Go long!" and makes a throw from the street. Brian misses the ball and it bounces onto the driveway, then rolls into the garage.

"Careful!" Erin shouts. "We're doing something critically important here."

"Yeah," Ethan says. "Doesn't sound like it's going too well."

Erin grits her teeth and actually growls.

"Um, I'll get the ball," I say. I hurl it to Ethan.

He grins as it goes right to him. "Wow, nice throw! Perfect spiral! Where'd you learn to throw like that, Zoe?"

I press a hand to my heart. Oh my God. "My dad, actually. He played football in high school."

"I didn't know that. Cool! You like football?"

"Yeah! I'm a big Bears fan."

Erin taps a Sharpie on the table. "Zoe! I asked you to hand me the eyedroppers."

"Oh, sorry."

"Are you with me here?"

"Of course!" I find the eyedroppers under a pile of papers, then hand them to Erin. "Anything changed since yesterday?" I ask.

She shakes her head sadly. "No. Nothing's working yet. But something will, I just know it."

I look over the row of small orange pots with the seedlings of invasive plants we placed into soil. We'd hoped one of the substances would stop their growth, but so far, they're proving to be indestructible. Every single plant is growing wildly.

“We have more elements to start testing today.” Erin looks at her list and points to some bottles and jars. “Sea salt, vinegar, peppermint, vanilla. We need to try as many as possible, don’t you think?”

“Definitely.” I steal a look at Ethan. That blue shirt really brings out his blue eyes. And the adorable sloppy way his shoes are always untied . . .

Erin clears her throat.

“Hi,” I say.

“Focus.”

“I am.”

She puts a seedling into a new pot, packs it with soil, and then I add a few drops of vinegar. I’m labeling the pot with a Sharpie when I hear Ethan shout, “Heads up!” and a second later, the football slams into the middle of the table.

I gasp. Everything goes flying. Ethan and Brian rush into the garage and Erin screams as several of our pots fall over onto their sides. A pitcher of water spills. I try to grab the eyedroppers but they roll off the table, hit the garage floor, and break. In a few seconds, our Invention Day project, our entire experiment, is a mess of wet papers, scattered seedlings, and overturned pots, with dirt covering everything in sight.

Erin makes a little sobbing noise as she brings her hands to her cheeks and stares wide-eyed at the table. She slowly turns to Ethan. "You did this on purpose, didn't you? To get me back. Because of what I said . . . that I thought you couldn't do it . . . that you don't have what it takes."

Ethan grabs the football. "No, I swear! It was an accident!"

She starts to cry, then angrily brushes away her tears. "An accident? I don't think so. You were aiming for the table."

He swallows, doesn't answer.

I put my arm around her. "It'll be okay. We can fix it, Erin."

"No." She sniffles. "Look at this. We can't."

Brian picks up a sheet of paper, shakes it, and lets water drip onto the floor. "It's my fault, really. I was the one who missed the ball."

Erin drags the back of her hand across her nose and looks at Ethan. "You know how important this was to me. You know how much I wanted to take first this year. Beat Marlon. And you sign up on a whim, when this isn't even your thing, and fool around with that junk in the basement like this is all one big joke?"

Ethan starts picking up the pots and brushing dirt off the table. "I'm sorry. Look, it's not so bad. We'll just clean up a little."

"Don't bother." Erin walks toward the door to their house, then turns around. "This is it. You and I. We're done." She goes inside. The door makes a little *click* sound that echoes through the garage.

Ethan slaps his hand onto his forehead. "It wasn't on purpose, I swear!"

I kneel next to the broken eyedroppers and pick up the glass pieces, then put them into the garbage can. "I know."

"I'm really sorry, Zoe," Ethan says. "I totally blew Invention Day for you."

I shrug, then sigh. "Nothing we were doing was working anyway. It was a good theory, though."

He gives me a sad smile. "Same thing's happening to us."

Brian says he's sorry too, then awkwardly shuffles his feet. "Uh . . . Maybe I should go, let you and your sister work this whole thing out." He backs away, then turns and hurries down the driveway.

"I'll get some paper towels," Ethan says. He goes into their house and comes back a minute later.

Then it's just me and Ethan in the garage. He tears off some paper towels and starts wiping the table. I realize I've never actually been alone with him before. Erin or Brian or someone else is always around, or we're in school with a hundred other people.

We're on opposite sides of the table, and we reach for the pitcher at the same time. Our hands touch. The hairs on my arm bristle. Then my heart thumps wildly and I get sweaty and tongue-tied and nervous and can barely look at him.

This is how it is when you're in love, you know. I've been reading.

I sneak a glance. He's looking at me, too. Oh! Should I tell him I love him, right here and right now? Maybe he feels the same! What if he does?! But is this a good moment, with what just happened? Help.

"Uh, Zoe?" he says.

"Yes?" I feel a little light-headed and sort of sway a bit.

"Are you okay?" He reaches out an arm to steady me.

"Um, yes, I'm fine. What did you want to say?"

He scratches the back of his neck. "Maybe you could talk to Erin for me? She's not gonna talk to me. This is bad. Worse than the waffles."

"What?"

"Nothing. Tell her I feel horrible about what happened, and I can, like, get whatever you need to fix your project. I'll pay for it and everything."

"Okay . . ."

"So you'll talk to her?"

I nod. "Sure. Anything else?"

He sighs. "Just—"

My heart leaps. "Yes?"

"Thanks, I guess."

"Of course." Then this pops out of my mouth: "Maybe when Erin isn't mad at you anymore, we can all go to a movie or something. . . ."

He shrugs. "Maybe."

Wasn't exactly the answer I was hoping for, but I'll take it.

CHAPTER TWENTY-ONE

What's Done Is Done

ERIN

There are no accidents, only some purpose we don't understand yet.

Have you ever heard that saying?

I think it fits this situation perfectly. Except for one major difference. I *do* understand the purpose. My brother wanted to ruin my Invention Day project. I called his bluff—told him he couldn't make his little desk-evator—and he retaliated because he knows I'm right.

No, I'm not being dramatic. I mean, how would you feel if that happened to you? Several weeks of work, over. Everything I planned, all of our theories, my detailed research notes—gone. Impossible to repair. It would take days just to reconstruct everything! And truthfully, I don't have the heart. It was crushed the moment the stupid football hit the table.

How can we go on? I'm afraid that Zoe and I will have to withdraw from Invention Day. Marlon will win. Again. And every day for the rest of the year, I'll have to live with that.

And Zoe, the ridiculous way she's acting around my brother. I can't even go there.

Am I really done with Ethan, like I said in the garage?

What do you think?

ETHAN

I swear, I didn't make a bad throw on purpose. I didn't aim for the table. I didn't secretly hope Brian would miss the ball, either, even though I know his skills need work. Is that what you think? No, no, no.

I could tell Erin those things a thousand times, but she wouldn't listen, and even if she did, she wouldn't believe me.

Yeah, I was mad because of what she said, sure, but it was an accident. Honest, times a million.

She looked completely crushed. Like all the air went out of her lungs. I've seen her look like that only a couple of other times. One was that day we missed the flight coming home. Another was when Romanov won last year's Invention Day.

This is worse than both of those put together.

So now we've gone from bonding over tomato soup to living in opposite galaxies to grating turning into hating.

I could try to fix it, like I told Zoe. Put everything back in order, get them new supplies, all that. But I know my sister. She'd say something like, "It's over. What's done is done."

She always makes everything so much more than it is. Even if it is.

BRIAN

Did I intentionally miss the ball? Is that what you're hinting at?

Erin's not my favorite person in the world, sure. That's pretty clear. But even I wouldn't stoop that low. Really. I wouldn't miss the ball on purpose. Hey, did you hear me? I said I wouldn't do that.

I'll tell you this, though. I don't want to say she

deserves it exactly, but maybe this'll make her see that not everything goes so perfect all the time.

Like me being one of the shortest guys in seventh grade. And the fact that I may never get Jamie Pappas to like me. Mom embarrassing me wherever we go. And puking on that roller coaster, then having everyone in line yell at me because they had to close the ride down.

Things happen, right? Deal with it. Crack a joke and be the first one to laugh. That's my strategy.

Gram had to move in with us now because she can't live by herself anymore. She tells the same stories over and over about when she was a girl in Poland and life wasn't so great there. It's impossible to follow where she's going with the stories. There's no beginning or end. Just a long, *long* middle.

Sometimes, though, she does seem to wrap it up, usually by putting down her teacup and clutching my hand and saying, "We didn't know, but it was a blessing in disguise."

And I go, "Glad it worked out, Gram."

So here's what I think about Ethan and Erin. The

ongoing Marcus vs. Marcus battle. What happened with the football was a blessing in disguise. Maybe it was a good thing, you know? Because now it's all finally out in the open. No more pretending. They can't stand each other and that's that.

CHAPTER TWENTY-TWO

Seagulls, Continued

WESLEY

Mom calls again on Sunday night. I won't talk to her. When Dad hangs up, he says that if I don't want to talk to Mom or him, maybe I'd like to talk to "someone."

I pull on the hood of my sweatshirt. "I don't need to do that."

After I say that, his face looks sad and defeated, like I punched him in the stomach. I hate when he looks like that. He didn't used to look like that.

So I go, "Dad. There's this teacher at school I talk to, okay?"

His face lights up, like this is excellent news. "I'm glad you're talking to someone." He pats my shoulder. "I'm here if you need me, Wes. I hope you know that."

"Yeah . . . I do."

Then he trashes the "moment" by giving me a replay

of Brett's wrestling match and I pull back, stop listening, tune him out. He still doesn't get that I don't want to hear about it.

But he suddenly stops talking. In the middle of a sentence.

"Sorry." He shrugs, like maybe he does get it. First time that's happened. "What's the teacher's name?"

"Gilardi."

"Which class does she teach?"

"I know her from Reflection."

"Oh." He smiles. "Okay."

I've thought a lot about Gilardi. And I think the reason I'm okay with her is because she never made me talk or asked me to share my feelings or any forced crap like that. If that makes sense. She's just there. I can go if I want, or skip it when I don't feel like talking.

And I'm gonna tell you something, okay, and don't repeat this to anyone. She kind of reminds me of my mom. They don't look alike or sound the same. It's just how Gilardi looks at me. Like no matter what I say, she's still gonna be there the next time I walk in.

So Monday after school, I decide to come clean. I walk

around Gilardi's room and tell her about Mom. How she left, how I haven't talked to her in months, and how I don't feel like talking to her ever again.

I've never told anyone what happened. Not that I have many people to tell. It feels a little good and a lot bad to say it all out loud. Not all. I leave out the part about Mom's friend. Or boyfriend.

Gilardi's sitting at her desk knitting, nodding and going "hmm" and "oh." But then she says, "This is tough, but you'll get through it," and "Try to see it as half-full, not half-empty." All that supposed-to-be-uplifting stuff. But instead of making me feel better, it's making me angry. At myself or Mom or the entire situation. I don't know anymore.

I stop in front of Gilardi, my hands in tight fists. "You can tell me all that, but you don't know what it's like. She takes off, doesn't care about me, or my brother. Thinks we're just gonna go live with her in Florida because that's what *she* wants? What if my parents end up fighting for custody and they never ask what *we* want? This is so frickin' messed up. People are so frickin' messed up."

Gilardi puts down her knitting, then takes off her

glasses and rubs her eyes. "You're right. It is messed up."

"Why'd my mom have to do this? It was fine before! We were okay!" I choke up a little and turn away so she won't see.

"I'm guessing she wasn't happy with her life."

"But it seemed like she was. If that's true, she was a great pretender."

"You don't ever really know what's going on inside someone, do you? My mother used to say, put yourself in someone else's shoes for a day and you'll want your own shoes back real fast."

"At least you had a mother to tell you stuff like that."

"True. She didn't leave. But I had other things."

"Like what? Your parents split? Your brother thought choke holds were a fun activity?"

She slides on her glasses, then stands and faces me. "No. I lost my sister. She died when she was four years old. I was seven."

I kick the leg of a desk. "Well, that sucks."

"It did indeed suck. She had leukemia. My parents and I were never the same afterward. The point is, everyone has hidden scars. Some people have deeper ones that take longer to heal, others not so much."

"But you got through it." I gesture around the room. "You're a teacher. You came out okay. Not everybody does, and you can't tell me that's not true."

"I won't. Some people can't get over things. You're right."

I slump into a chair. "So how do you know if you're gonna come out okay? Because a lot of the time, it doesn't feel like I will."

She picks up whatever she's been knitting and smiles. "I don't know if this scarf's going to come out okay."

I know she's trying to get me to laugh, but I don't want to. Then I'd have to open the door even farther, and a little was hard enough.

"Let's go back to those seagulls for a minute," she says. "There was a time when they made a choice to leave the water and go inland. For whatever reason. Food, avoiding their predators, better places to build nests. But I'm certain they didn't know at first if it was going to come out okay."

"They're only seagulls. They can't think. What does it matter anyway?"

"It matters. Of course it matters."

I get up, go over to the window, look out on nothing. "What are you saying?"

"I think you know."

I smirk. "I'm supposed to leave the water and go inland?"

She laughs. "I guess that's one way to put it."

"And then it'll all be okay?"

"No. But it's a place to start."

I don't say anything.

"You decide, Wesley. It's become a tired cliché, but that's the one thing you can do here. The one thing in your control."

CHAPTER TWENTY-THREE

Status Update

ZOE

Tuesday during lunch, I try to talk to Erin like Ethan asked me to, but she gets super mad and turns on me. She tells me I'm "taking his side." I promise her I'm not and I'm just trying to help smooth things out, but then she goes, "Zoe, can't you see he made a bad throw on purpose? It was clear he aimed for the table. He wanted to destroy our project."

I say no, I don't think that's how it was, Ethan wouldn't do that. She crosses her arms and shakes her head. "You don't know," she says. "You don't know how he really is. No one does."

I keep trying, but she plugs her ears like a little kid and won't listen. And I realize that no matter what I say, she's got her mind made up.

That's when I get mad.

"Stop blaming him!" I shout. "It *was* an accident! Admit it, what you're really upset about is how our project wasn't working! I'm upset too, but that doesn't mean we should give up!"

Her hands are folded tightly in her lap and she won't look at me.

"If we have to start over, that's okay. Our world is in peril! Sea levels are rising! Polar ice is melting! And invasive plants are a threat to biodiversity and human health. We have to focus on that and not some little brother-sister argument!"

Finally she turns. "Nice speech, Zoe. But this isn't a *little* argument, and my brother has to realize that you can't just say you're sorry after you create a mess and then everything's fine."

"Erin, listen—"

She stands abruptly, gathers up her lunch. "And tell me the truth, you like him, don't you?"

I bite my lip. "Yes."

"I knew it." She walks to the garbage can, dumps

everything—not recycling even one item—then leaves the cafeteria.

Parneeta, sitting next to me, says, "What's going on with Erin?"

"It's a long story," I sigh. "And it doesn't have a happy ending."

BRIAN

Three amazing things happened today.

The first was in LA. I made a joke about Delman's tie: COMMAS SAVE LIVES. I said, "Unless you get stabbed by an exclamation point," and are you ready for this? Jamie laughed. She goes, "That was funny, Brian." I about died.

Two, the protein diet is working! I grew. Only one inch, according to the pencil marks on the kitchen wall, but I'm taking that to mean more inches are coming. Even Gram said I looked taller, and she seemed all there at that moment, not lost somewhere in one of her stories. I'm on an upward roll, I can feel it. Good-bye, shortness.

And three, I was invited to Naomi's Halloween party. She has one every year, but I never made the cut before. She's good friends with this girl Sheridan, who's friends with Jamie, so the only explanation I can come up with is that Jamie got me on the list.

Days don't get much better than this.

ETHAN

I have no idea if Zoe talked to my sister, because now Erin's not doing the thing where she speaks to me through Mom and Dad. She's acting as if I don't even exist.

In school, at home, on the bus, wherever. She walks right by me, staring straight ahead. Like she's never going to forgive me. She's sticking 100 percent to what she said in the garage—the "We're done" comment.

Mom and Dad know what's going on, but they told me they want us to "work it out on our own" because that's what you say when you're fully committed to Parenting 101.

I answered, "I'm willing, but it takes two, you know."

They said they understand, and I should give Erin

some time, that she's very hurt about what happened and it's still "raw."

"I said I was sorry. I offered to fix it and pay for whatever they needed." (Not that I have any money, so I don't know how that would happen.)

They said that was the right thing to do and they're sure it will be okay. Eventually.

Anyway, after a few days of waiting to see if she'd get over it, I kick open the door to her room one night. She's at her desk, hunched over something, most likely homework that I should be doing too. She does this sideways glance toward my feet.

I slap my hand on her dresser. "Look, I'm sorry! I don't know what else you want me to say. I can't erase what happened. You can hate me for the rest of your life if you want to. I guess that's your choice. But stop the silent treatment already. It's just stupid at this point, Erin."

She doesn't look up, doesn't say a word.

"And here." I pull a crumpled napkin from my pocket with a few mini marshmallows wrapped inside. I think they're stale, and I couldn't roast minis, but whatever. It's the gesture, right? I put the napkin onto her desk. One marshmallow rolls to the floor.

She glances at it. I wait for her to say something. She doesn't.

"Fine. No one can say I didn't try."

ERIN

I know he tried. Don't come down on me. See, this is what always happens. Ethan does something, but then somehow it ends up being my fault for getting mad. Don't you see how wrong that is? I can't even bear to walk into the garage.

I've forgiven him so many times before, or let it go, or not made a big issue. But this time is different. I was going to win this year. Take it away from Marlon Romanov. Then he could finally stop acting so smug and superior every time he passes me in the hallway.

You know that last year, after Marlon took first place, he walked up to me and said, "This is proof that men are better than girls at science."

I was so stunned, I couldn't even respond. Then he marched over to the judges to shake their hands and I watched. And yes, I cried. When I got home.

So I had something to prove this year, and it was bigger than me. It was for girls—women—everywhere.

Zoe's all upbeat and positive and thinks we can just pick up the pieces and go on. Plus, how could she like Ethan? That really hurts. And Mom and Dad keep suggesting that I need to find a way to get past this.

But I'm not able to do that right now.

It's not only the football incident, which is bad enough. Ethan went and asked Marlon for help. Not me.

I pick up the marshmallow from the floor. It's kind of hard. Stale, I'm sure. Where did he find these anyway?

I ball up the napkin and I'm about to throw them away, but then I eat every single one. I forgot how good marshmallows are, even if they're stale. And unroasted. There are times that can be okay.

WESLEY

Go inland. Like the seagulls. Sure. You do that and tell me how it goes.

At lunch, I sit where I always sit. The table with the kids who have nowhere else to sit. The guy with long hair who has his headphones on the whole time, three guys who do their homework, this heavy kid who gets two lunch trays. And me.

Every day.

I eat my sandwich, shut out the noise, watch the heavy kid go through all his food. The bell rings. I get up, walk to the trash can.

I didn't plan this. But Marcus is on the other side of the can, throwing his garbage away. He glances at me. I remember when he was in Reflection, how he was so nice and polite to Gilardi all the time. Some kids are pretty rude to her. And I just think, *Say something.*

So I tip my chin and go, "Hey."

And he says, "Hey. How's it goin'?"

"All right."

"Well, see ya." He leaves, walks out with Kowalski.

I think I'm the last one in the cafeteria. The monitor blows her whistle. "Get going, young man."

Yeah. Okay.

CHAPTER TWENTY-FOUR

Two Peas in a Pod

ETHAN

As soon as the bell rings on Friday afternoon, I head to Gilardi's room. I've decided I can't do it. I'm quitting. Giving up on the invention. I'm not the carrot seed kid after all. I made a decent attempt, but I guess I really don't have what it takes. Erin was right. Like always.

Last night I went down to the basement with a big garbage bag and packed up everything we used to try to make the desk-evator. Don't get me wrong. I still get scomas, and I still think that kids shouldn't be forced to sit at their desks all day and rule number seven needs to change. But I've got to face facts. I can't make this thing and never will. The desk-evator was a great idea, but thinking I could do Invention Day was a bad one.

It's time to go to Plan B. Or actually, Plan C.

As soon as I come up with it.

I don't even tell Brian. He won't care. Actually, he'll be happy. He didn't want to do this in the first place. All he can think about is Jamie anyway. Now he can focus on her full-time.

When I'm almost at Gilardi's room, I hear my sister's voice. "I don't see how we can," she says. "I feel as if I have no other choice."

What? I poke my head into the room and Erin's in there, standing in front of Gilardi's desk. Her back is to me. I quickly step back and duck out but too late. Gilardi spotted me. "Ethan? It's all right," she calls. "Come in. How funny, your sister's here too."

I cringe, then go inside. "Hi." That was to Gilardi, not Erin.

"What can I do for you?" Gilardi asks me.

"Well . . . ," I start, not sure if I want to say it in front of Erin. Then I think, *Whatever, doesn't matter, who cares at this point? It's all messed up anyway.* "Yeah, uh, I want to withdraw from Invention Day."

Gilardi puts a hand on her cheek. "Not you, too? That's just what your sister was telling me."

Erin and I actually give each other a brief, very brief glance.

"The thing is," I say, "my project sounded like a good plan, and I—we—thought we could make the desk-evator, but nothing we've tried is working."

Gilardi shakes her head. "You and your sister are two peas in a pod."

"We're not," Erin says immediately.

"We're really not," I add. "We're complete opposites. Different galaxies."

"Right," Erin echoes. "Oil and water. Day and night. Hot and cold."

"Fast and slow. Up"—I can't help but smile—"and down."

The corner of Erin's lip twitches, like she might want to smile too but she's holding it back. We lock eyes for a second, and then she looks away.

Gilardi ignores our little list of examples. "Erin was just saying that she's had some unexpected trouble with her project too, and she feels that she has no other choice but to withdraw. But here's what I'm going to say to both of you." Gilardi slides the pencil out of her hair bun and points it at us. "I'm not going to accept your withdrawals."

"What?" I blurt.

"Why not?" Erin asks.

"I think you both can do what you set out to do. If we don't fail, we don't learn. You know that. I ask you to sleep on it over the weekend. If you still want to withdraw your projects on Monday, I'll accept it then. But not now."

Sleep on it. Gilardi's solution for everything.

Erin shakes her head. "Ms. Gilardi, the thing is—"

She gets up. "Nope, no."

"I don't want to sleep on it," Erin says. "I've already made up my mind."

"Monday," Gilardi answers, shooing us out. "Things always look brighter after a good night's sleep. And you can quote me on that."

There's nothing else to do then except walk out. Sort of together. When we're in the hallway—which is deserted except for Wesley sitting on the floor, his back against a locker—Erin starts to walk away, then stops and turns around. "I want to tell you something."

"What?"

"You remember that best friend I had, Ellie? The one who moved away?"

"Kind of."

"That day we missed the flight because you were making waffles in the hotel, we were so late getting home, I never got to say good-bye to her."

I sigh. Oh man. "Why didn't you ever tell me that?"

"Because it wouldn't have changed anything."

"Okay, look. I'm just gonna say this. You shouldn't withdraw your project because of what happened with the football. I mean it. You were right about me. I'm the one who doesn't know what I'm doing. I'm sure you'll figure out a way to fix it. You always do."

"I don't think this is fixable."

"Listen, you and Zoe have a brilliant idea. The kind of idea that can really make a difference in the world."

She tilts her head, eyes me.

"I'm being serious," I say, and I swear I am. I hold up my palm like I'm taking an oath or something. "And sorry about your friend. Sorry about everything I ever did to you in my whole entire life. I hope that covers it."

She moves her backpack to the other shoulder. "Well . . . I'm going to wait for the late bus."

"Okay."

"You're walking?"

"Yeah."

She gives me this little smile. "Ethan . . . *Por supuesto no me equivocaba contigo.*"

Another subject my sister excels at: Spanish. "What?" I say.

"Figure it out."

"I'll never even remember what you said."

We both stand there for a few seconds, and then she leaves.

"Bye, Rin," I say under my breath. What I used to call her when we were little. When things weren't so complicated. When tomatoes and marshmallows were enough.

ERIN

That was nice of him. He didn't have to say all that.

There are times he can be okay.

There are times he's not such a bad brother. Or person.

So. I don't know.

WESLEY

I stand. "Hey, Marcus."

He looks at me. "Yeah?"

"You want to know what she said?"

"You know?"

"Yeah. Turns out, I'm kinda decent at Spanish."

"Okay."

"She said, 'Of course I was right about you.'"

Marcus shakes his head. "Thanks."

"Sure." I go inside Gilardi's room.

"Wesley," she says. "How was your day?"

CHAPTER TWENTY-FIVE

The Party

ERIN

I sleep on it like Ms. Gilardi suggested, but when I wake up Saturday morning, I still don't know what I should do. Or want to do. Anyway, it's Halloween, and tonight's Naomi's party, so this is very unlike me, but I'm not going to stress about it today.

Zoe and I were going to be eighties girls, but we're not exactly best friends at the moment. We haven't talked much since lunch on Tuesday. We're not *not* talking, but it's definitely been awkward. I'm still having trouble processing the fact that she likes my brother. And does he like her? I mean, that just brought everything to another level, you know?

So I guess I'll dress up as an eighties girl by myself.

I spend all morning looking up pictures online of eighties movie stars, then all afternoon making my hair big (which is easy) and splatter-painting an old sweatshirt. Mom gives me a pair of old neon-orange leg warmers she used to wear. I slather on lipstick and glittery eye shadow, put a headband around my forehead, and I'm set.

Mom laughs as she's taking a picture of me. "You look very rad, dudette. That's eighties slang for 'radical.'"

"Thanks?"

She wants to get a picture of me and Ethan together, but he won't put on his costume. He tells Mom he's keeping it a secret and isn't showing anyone until he gets to Naomi's house. In the car on the way there, Dad's the only one who talks.

"So a Halloween party, huh?"

"Glad kids still do this sort of thing."

"I bet you won't be bobbing for apples and carving pumpkins, though. What do kids do at Halloween parties these days?"

Ethan's looking out the window and I'm doing the same. Dad keeps talking, telling us a story about his cousin, who once whipped a giant jawbreaker at someone's house when they were trick-or-treating and hit their mailbox and made a dent. "At high speed," he says, "those things are like meteors."

We pull up at Naomi's house. Dad turns around to us and grins. "So my advice is to stay away from giant jawbreakers. And mailboxes."

"You're so weird, Dad," I say.

Ethan gets out. "Bye. See you later."

Brian's waiting for Ethan outside. They throw their arms around each other and get into a huddle. About their costumes, probably. I ring the doorbell but no one answers, so I just go in.

Tons of people are already there. A lot of the theater kids that Naomi's friends with. Sheridan and Jacob and this guy Armando, who's wearing a Mr. Potato Head costume that everyone thinks is hysterical.

I spot Zoe across the room. She isn't an eighties girl. She and Parneeta are dressed as winter and summer, apparently. Zoe's hair is spray-painted yellow and she's wearing a green tank top, jean shorts, sunglasses, and flip-flops. Parneeta's got on an ugly Christmas sweater, a knitted hat, and mittens.

I get a little catch in my throat. Zoe glances at me, and suddenly I feel stupid for sticking to the eighties idea when she didn't.

She's hanging with Parneeta and Jamie, so I get a cup of punch from a giant bowl with fake steam coming off the top, then stand next to a bookcase, not knowing what to do or who to talk to or anything.

Naomi's mom is walking around with a tray of bloody fingers made out of cookie dough and red icing, telling everyone she found the recipe on Pinterest and isn't it cool? Armando starts doing karaoke, singing that friend song from *Toy Story*. Jacob's tossing M&Ms into the air and catching them in his mouth.

Then suddenly Armando stops singing, points, and starts cracking up. Everyone turns and looks toward the door. Ethan and Brian make their entrance.

They're sumo wrestlers.

I should've known it would be something like this.

They have on giant inflatable skin-colored costumes with a black strip around the middle that looks like a tiny pair of shorts and black caps with a fake hair bun attached. They walk, actually more like waddle, toward the center of the room and everyone crowds around them, taking pictures and bumping into them and patting the fake buns.

I mean, everyone except me. I'm still by the bookcase.

Brian and Ethan go over to the karaoke machine and pick up the microphones and start doing a kind of rap. Which is really just a lot of grunting and pretending to make muscles, but everyone loves it, even Naomi's mom, who's clapping along and also making muscles.

Jamie's standing near me. "Your brother's hilarious," she says. "Is he like this all the time?"

"Yes. No. I don't know."

Jamie looks at me and tilts her head, then sort of drifts away, and for some reason, I think of the time when Ethan and I went to her birthday party in third grade. There was a magician, and of course, he asked for volunteers. Who volunteers first? Right, my brother.

Anyway, he went up there and pretty much stole the show. He was right on cue with the jokes and even did his own trick, pulling a quarter from behind the guy's ear. The magician said, "Hey, kid, you want to quit school and go on the road with me?"

And Ethan answered, "Sure, how much you gonna pay me?"

I remember watching him then like I'm watching him now. I would never do those kinds of things. I don't like when I'm embarrassed or put on the spot or people are laughing, because I never quite know if it's with me or at me.

But Ethan . . . None of that bothers him.

I like who I am, I really do. I have a lot of good qualities and I don't have self-esteem issues, so don't jump to that conclusion.

But can I tell you something? Just once, or maybe even more than once, I'd like to have someone say I'm hilarious. But not if it involves wearing a sumo wrestler costume.

CHAPTER TWENTY-SIX

The Mystery

ETHAN

Monday morning on the bus, I tell Brian I'm going to withdraw our project from Invention Day.

He blows out a breath. "Excellent decision. I'm not saying I told you so . . . but I am."

"It's fine, you can say it. We stink at inventions."

"But we're brilliant at being pretend sumo wrestlers."

"True. Maybe we can dress up in the sumo costumes and do a karaoke song for D'Antonio about how kids shouldn't be chained to their desks. Whaddya think?"

Brian leans away, practically out of the seat. "You're on your own with that one."

"I wasn't serious."

"Good. I was a little worried there for a second."

I sigh. "You know the worst part about this whole thing? Nothing's ever gonna change. Radical protest: fail.

Cool invention: fail. So I'll be sitting in school until I'm old and fat and my muscles have wasted away to the point where I couldn't stand at my desk even if I wanted to."

"Sucks, I know, but like my Gram says, it is what it is."

"Yeah . . ."

"Or like she also says, never put potatoes under the bed."

I laugh. "Okay. Good to know. You want all your stuff back, by the way? The Slinkys and everything?"

Brian grins and pats my back. "You can keep it all, dude." He flutters his eyelashes. "Our special memory."

"Thanks."

When we get to school, I trudge to my locker. Another week of classes. Another week of same old, same old.

There are eight minutes until the bell, just enough time to get to Gilardi's room and tell her I slept on it and I'm for sure withdrawing. Except when I open my locker, a white paper, folded into quarters, falls out. I pick it up and unfold it.

There are only a few words on the paper, and they're typed:

think about how a folding table works

What?

I check around to see if anyone's watching me, but no one is. At least not that I notice. Who the heck wrote this, and why? How did they know where my locker is? And what's it supposed to mean?

Think about how a folding table works?

Do you have a clue here? Because I certainly don't.

Erin comes to her locker, right next to mine, opens it, and hangs up her jacket.

I go, "Hi."

She takes out some folders, gives me a sideways glance. "I just saw you at breakfast, but okay, hi."

"What's going on?"

"Um. Nothing." She shuts her locker and leaves.

Was it her? How could it be? She just got here. How could she have put the note in my locker?

I refold the paper and slide it into the back pocket of my jeans. Then the bell rings and it's too late to go to Gilardi's room. I'll have to go after school.

I rush to math, take my seat, and start working on the warm-up problem on the board, but really, the only thing in my head is the mysterious note.

All lowercase letters, no period. Typed. Erin would

never write a sentence without proper punctuation, although she would definitely type it. Unless she was trying to throw me off so I wouldn't think it was her. She'd do that.

But anyway, why would someone write that and put it in my locker? What does it mean? I finish the math problem and plunk my pencil down. Someone's trying to tell me something! But about . . . a folding table? Maybe that's a clue for something else. A secret message or an encrypted code.

At lunch I show the note to Brian. He doesn't have any answers either and thinks the note wasn't even meant for me but was put into the wrong locker by mistake.

"It's probably part of someone's homework or something," he says, then resumes his constant staring at Jamie, who's sitting across the cafeteria. "Should I just ask her out already?"

"I don't know."

"There's solid evidence she likes me."

"Like what?"

"At the party, she talked to me for practically an hour!"

"Yeah, in a group with about five other people."

"So! Plus, she loved the sumo costume."

I shrug, finish my sandwich. Slowly scan the cafeteria to see if anyone's looking my way. Nope.

It doesn't come to me until I'm scomatizing in LA that the note might have something to do with the desk-evator. I bolt up in my chair. What if someone's trying to help me? Give me a tip of some sort? Would someone do that?

Not that many people know about my idea. Erin, Zoe, Romanov, Gilardi, Mom and Dad. I told a few kids at the Halloween party too. They were all like, don't give up, you gotta do this. So maybe it was one of them? Sheridan? Parneeta? I can't even remember who else was around when I was talking about it.

Suddenly I realize Delman's drumming his fingers on my desktop. Everyone in the room is quiet. I look up.

"Ethan," he says. "I asked you to explain how the second stanza in the poem contributes to its overall meaning."

"The second stanza?" I repeat, quickly reading it on the whiteboard. "Sorry, uh, I don't know."

Delman sighs, then turns away and calls on my sister, who of course has her hand raised. "It relates to the theme of loneliness," she answers. "How we can never really know another person. We're all just oil and water, not ever truly understanding each other."

Delman nods. "Interesting way to put it, but yes."

Erin glances at me, as if she wasn't talking about the poem, but . . . her and me.

And I get this weird feeling that she wrote the note. Maybe she felt bad about what she said in Spanish and she's not mad anymore and is trying to secretly help me. But in typical Erin style, it's not easy to figure out.

It's not until school's over and I'm walking to Gilardi's room that it comes to me. I stop in the middle of the hallway and take the note from my pocket. I'm a complete idiot. It *is* about the desk-evator. She's telling me that instead of the sides raising up like an elevator, I should make it like a *folding table* with legs that fold in. Duh, duh, duh.

I run out the front door while texting Brian. **It isn't over yet. A miracle just happened.**

CHAPTER TWENTY-SEVEN

The Desk-evator

ETHAN

I run toward home, texting Brian to get to my house ASAP. I tear through the park, the seagulls scattering and shrieking, then sprint the last few blocks like this is a race and I'm nearing the finish line.

This is a race! A race to eliminate scomas! To save myself and every kid in every school everywhere.

When I reach my house, I punch in the code on the number pad outside the garage, then duck under when it's not even fully open. Everything's exactly the same as the day Zoe and I tried to clean up the mess. But what I want to see is the table. The *folding* table.

I crawl underneath to see how the legs are attached. It's a little more complicated than I imagined. On each of the four corners, there's a hinge (yeah, okay, I learned something from my trip to Home Depot) and a screw and a slide-y type metal thing. Technical term for that last one.

"Okay, I'm here," Brian says. "What's up, dude? What's the miracle?"

I quickly scoot out from under the table, leap up, and slap the top. "This is how we do it! This is how we make the desk-evator. It doesn't raise up, it has legs that fold in and out. Like a *stand*, so we can stand. Get it?"

"Ah," he says. "Clever. Why didn't we think of that?"

"Because we were so stuck on doing it the other way."

"So that's what the person who wrote the note was telling you?"

"I think."

"But who wrote it?"

"Doesn't matter. It's someone who obviously wants to help us! Let's not question it, let's just go with it. Whaddya say?"

He groans. "I thought we were quitting, that this nightmare was behind us."

"We're not. Come on." I grab Brian's arm and drag him inside, then go directly to the pile of bags that Mom left in the laundry room, ready to drop off at Goodwill. One is filled with old kitchen stuff. Just yesterday, she was cleaning out the kitchen! And right on top of the bag is a scratched-up, half-broken cutting board.

Exactly what we need.

From the kitchen drawers, I grab four chip clips, a roll of duct tape, two wooden spoons, and two spatulas. Not stuff that's going to Goodwill. Stuff we're still using. But Mom won't mind if I borrow them for a while, will she? Not for a good reason, I'm sure.

Brian's leaning against the counter with his arms crossed. "Looks like you're on a mission."

"You bet I am." I go down to the basement, carrying all the stuff, and Brian follows.

I tape the spoons and spatulas to the corners of the cutting board at ninety degree angles, then tape the chip clips onto the bottom of each spoon/spatula. And in less than ten minutes, I've got the desk-evator pretty much put together. It folds and unfolds. It clips. After all those fails, it just happens.

Was it like this for Edison? Thousands of light bulbs that didn't succeed, then one day, something worked.

This is that day. Me and Thomas E, we've got something in common now.

I try to stand it up on the floor. So it looks like a preschool art project gone bad, and the thing's kind of unstable. I have to hold on to it, but it's okay. It gets the message across.

Erin *wasn't* right about me.

"Behold the desk-evator," I announce. "It can be folded up and stacked in the back of a classroom. When you can't sit anymore, you go get one, unfold it, clip it onto your desk, and bam! You can stand, stretch your legs, take a quiz, take notes, whatever."

Brian's nodding. "I like it. It has a very . . . homemade kitchen-type look."

"This is only a prototype, of course." I smooth down one corner of the tape. "Maybe I can use some hinges."

"Hinges? Whoa. Who are you?"

"Oh, just an inventor." I grin, then tilt my head and look at it. "I made this thing. What if it takes off and I get a patent and it actually gets used in schools? I mean, this could really be big—"

Brian fake-coughs. "Hold on. This isn't going to win, Ethan, you know that, right?"

I shrug.

"Come on. I heard Romanov's working on a robotic hand that you control through an app. That's what wins invention fairs, not this."

"You don't know that for sure."

"Uh, yeah, I do."

"Well, this is what we got, and we're going with it. It solves a real problem. Something important." I pull my phone from my pocket and take a few pictures of the desk-evator, then print them for the middle section of the display board.

Brian goes, "Hey, I'd use it. I'm just saying."

I look at my invention, lying on its side. "The thing is, you gotta believe, you know? If you don't, what's the point?"

What's the point of planting a carrot seed in the first place if you don't believe it'll come up?

"I guess so," Brian says. "Okay, you want me to make the diagram of how it's supposed to work? We had to do that, right?"

"Yeah, good idea."

While he's sketching, I go upstairs and get the pictures from Dad's printer, then glue them onto the board. When Brian's finished, he adds the drawing. We prop the desk-evator next to the display board and stand back. One of the spatulas pops off and I retape it.

"We might want to think about those hinges," Brian says.

"Maybe. But people will get the general idea of what we're aiming for here, right? The concept."

"Well, I'll say this. We should definitely bring some duct tape to Invention Day."

ERIN

I'm sitting at the top of the basement stairs. I've been listening. Hmm. Interesting.

Now they're goofing around, laughing and pounding on something (the air hockey table?) and doing some sort of rap. But this time it's not about sumo wrestling, it's about their invention.

I hear Brian shout, "School got rules, that we know!" Then Ethan comes in: "But McNutt number seven has got to go!"

Then they make this *ch-ch-ch* sound and crack up.

I draw up my knees and wrap my arms around them. Close my eyes. Keep listening.

My brother can barely get out the words: "Sit, sit, sit, (laugh) there goes your (laugh) brain. Sit some more, you (laugh) go insane."

More cracking up. Then it sounds like they're running around the basement, playing kickball or basketball or something ball.

I stand, get my backpack from the kitchen, and go upstairs. I pull out my math folder, then write my name on the worksheet that's due tomorrow.

This morning I was all ready to tell Ms. Gilardi that I'm withdrawing from Invention Day. I was on the way to her room. I was going to, I really was. But then I didn't. You want to know why? The reason I didn't withdraw? I can't answer that, because I don't know.

I don't like when that happens. When I'm unclear and foggy about a decision. It doesn't happen a lot, only once in a while.

Dad's convinced I'll make a good accountant one day, like him. He always tells me I'm a natural problem solver and never fail to see the forest for the trees, which means I don't get bogged down in small details and I grasp the big picture.

Except, what would he say now?

By the way, not that I want to keep dwelling on Waffle Day, but I never told you something else that happened.

Ethan made me a waffle.

It had strawberries on top in the shape of a smiley face.

It was delicious.

CHAPTER TWENTY-EIGHT

Substitute Friend

ZOE

Since Erin and I are, well, you know, sort of in a fight, I've been hanging out with Parneeta. She's okay. Some of the time. Actually, she's completely obsessed with shopping. And fashion. And mostly, makeup.

She's done a makeover on me three times, not that I thought I needed even one. But she insisted I did. One look for day, one for evening, and one for special occasions. She knows the names of things I've never heard of, like primer, luminizer, and bronzer. She was surprised I didn't know what these are, and keeps telling me if I wore makeup, I'd be gorgeous.

I never thought about being gorgeous. I look how I look, and I'm okay with it. Plus, there are so many more important things to worry about in the world. You know me by now, so I don't have to list them.

Anyway, we're at her house on Friday night, in her room, and she's painting her nails a color called caterpillar. After she's done, she wants to paint mine, but I'm not sure how I feel about lime-green fingernails. Or a nail polish company choosing the name of an essential insect for this color. It kind of demeans the caterpillar, don't you think?

Parneeta spins around on the stool at her makeup table. "Do you want to know how many eye shadow palettes I have?"

"You counted them?"

She giggles. "I did. I got two new ones this week with my babysitting money. So, how many, do you think?"

"I don't know."

"Eleven!"

"Wow. How do you wear that many eye shadows?"

She blows on her nails. "Oh, that's easy. I wear a different one every day. I can try some on you if you want. You'd look really good in this color from Urban Decay."

"No, that's okay." I see something that looks like a cross between a nylon back sack and a regular backpack on the floor by her bed. It's a shiny pink zebra-print fabric, and there are a bunch of pockets and pouches.

"Is this your Invention Day project?" I ask. I'd heard she was making some kind of backpack.

"Uh-huh. You can try it out if you want to."

I pick it up, put it on. "It's really light. I mean, there's nothing in it, but still."

"Yeah, that's one of the selling points—it's made from parachute fabric. It'll put an end to kids having sore backs and shoulders from heavy backpacks. But I'll tell you a secret. My real reason for doing this is that backpacks are so ugly. I wanted to design something sturdy, weightless, and stylish."

I take it off and examine it. "Did you sew this?"

She shrugs. "My mom helped on that part. She's, like, an amazing sewer. She used to make all my clothes, but now I mostly get stuff at the mall. You know. Anyway, I'm ready for you!"

I try protesting, but I end up with lime-green fingernails. And toes. And the Urban Decay eye shadow on my lids. It makes me look like I have two black eyes.

That's why I'm really, really, REALLY glad when Erin texts and tells me that she's sorry. Can you come over tomorrow? she asks. We can pick up where we left off with our project. Okay?

I reply right away. YES! What time?

Ten?

I'll be there.

Great. Thanks.

Can't wait! So happy! I do a gazillion smiling emojis.

Then it's like this tsunami of relief washes over me. Not that I'm making light of tsunamis or anything, they're quite serious. I'm just so HAPPY!

While I was typing, I messed up the polish on my thumbs. Parneeta says she can redo them, but I tell her it's okay. I'm going to take the polish off as soon as I get home anyway.

I quickly say bye, it's been fun, and wish her good luck at Invention Day. "See you there!" I say, and text Mom to pick me up immediately.

CHAPTER TWENTY-NINE

The Discovery

ERIN

Zoe's not an on-time person. She always gets wrapped up in something she's doing or forgets to check the time or stops to help someone who's lost. I'm used to it. I expect it, and I plan for it.

But on Saturday morning, at exactly ten a.m., her face is pressed against the window next to my front door.

When I open it, she grabs me in a tight hug. "I missed you! I'm so glad you texted!"

I pull back after a few seconds. "I missed you too. And . . . I'm sorry I got so mad. About everything."

"Me too! I'm sorry too."

I glance upstairs. Ethan's still sleeping. "You can like my brother if you want to," I whisper. "It's all right."

She squeezes my arm, then hugs me again.

"Okay, okay," I say. "Don't get all mush ball on me. We have a lot of work to do."

She wipes her eyes and sniffles. "I can't help it! So, are we good now?"

"We're good." I point to her fingernails, which have a weird tinge of green. "You polished your nails? You never do that."

She shakes her head. "Parneeta. Caterpillar."

"What?"

"Forget it. Not important." She hooks her arm through mine. "Let's go find a way to destroy those invasive plants!"

We walk arm in arm toward the garage. I take a deep breath as I slowly open the door. This'll be the first time I've been in there since the . . . *incident*.

For days Mom's been asking me to clean up everything if I'm not going to continue with the experiment. She said it's getting chilly and she'd like the garage back, please, for her car and Dad's.

"I understand what you've been going through," she told me, "but enough is enough already."

I thought that was a little harsh, but then I realized it's been two weeks.

I flip on the light, and Zoe and I walk over to the table. It's the same as I remember. A disorganized mess of seedlings, bottles, branches, leaves, pots, dirt. But at least now, everything's dry.

"Ethan and I tried to straighten up a little," Zoe says. "The day it happened."

I pick up my pad of paper. Most of my notes on the top page are water-stained, but some are still readable.

"Where should we start?" Zoe asks.

I look around. "I'm not sure. . . ."

"Okay, well." Zoe gently takes my notepad. "Let's see, we recorded data for the first batch of substances. The elderberry and tea tree oil and all those. And none seemed to have an effect on the invasive plants. But the later things we tried? What were they? Oh here, it's in your notes, of course! Peppermint, vinegar, sea salt, vanilla. I don't think we examined the plants when those were added."

"Right. We didn't have a chance."

Zoe starts picking up some of the pots and looking at the labels. "Here's the peppermint. Oh, I think the seedling fell out. And most of the dirt too. We'll have to do this one again. I hope we have time."

She keeps picking up pots and talking, but I'm sifting through the tiny tangled roots that are lying on one end of the table. Something's weird. Something's not right. Or is right. My heart leaps. No, it isn't possible.

I run toward the door to the house, then push it open so hard that it bangs against the wall in the laundry room.

"Erin?" Zoe calls.

"I'll be right back!"

I rush up the stairs, almost crashing into Ethan on his way down.

"Wha?" he says, scratching his head.

"Sorry!" I shout, then tear into my room and rifle through my desk drawers. In less than thirty seconds, I've got my magnifying glass in hand and I'm on my way back downstairs.

Ethan's in the kitchen, pouring milk into a bowl. Life cereal, like always. He squints at me. "What's going on?"

"No time to talk!"

I go into the garage, then stop and take a few breaths before I walk to the table to see if what I think is true is really true.

Ethan pokes his head into the garage.

Zoe waves. "Hi, Ethan!"

I quickly turn and motion for him to stay inside. "Don't come in here."

"I won't do anything, I promise. No footballs."

"No. We have a ton of work to do. And very little time."

He yawns. "Can I at least stand here?"

"You cannot." I shake my head, then close the door. I hear him say "Jeez" as I take small, even, trying-to-be-calm steps to the table.

Zoe's watching me. "Erin, what's—"

I put my finger to my lips, then hold the magnifying glass over the roots. Zoe comes around the table and stands next to me.

I bend down and examine them closely, turning them over and looking at them from different angles. Finally I lower the magnifying glass and stand up straight.

"What is it?" Zoe asks, her eyes wide.

"Some of the roots," I say, "are different. Sort of shriveled, and lighter in color, almost like they were, I don't know, bleached out."

Zoe gasps. "But from what? Which substance made that happen?"

"I don't know."

"This is amazing!" Zoe cries. "Something worked?"

"It's possible. It's entirely possible."

She dances around the table, then grabs my hands and spins us in a circle. "Erin! Do you understand that we could be on the brink of a discovery that will save thousands of endangered plant forms worldwide?"

"I—I can't believe it."

She jumps and claps. "Me neither!"

But then I realize something. I have no idea how to proceed. What to do next. This wasn't how I planned for our project to go. An accidental discovery with no clue how it happened? Now what?

Then I realize something else. Without my brother throwing the football and without Brian missing it, this might not have happened.

It *was* an accident.

Ethan, in his Ethan-ness, was the one who made our experiment work.

CHAPTER THIRTY

Sunday Dinners

WESLEY

Dad calls me to come down for dinner. He made spaghetti and meatballs. The guy keeps trying, I gotta give him credit for that. He's not giving up on us. I would've given up a long time ago.

I can't take how Mom's chair at the table is empty. The three of us sit, and it's like the chair is waiting for her. As if she's gonna come back. Just walk in the door. Maybe tonight, and she'll sit down with us and joke about things like she used to. How Brett's hair sticks up in the morning and makes him look deranged, and how my laugh sounds like Bart Simpson's. How we finish eating before she takes two bites.

How she's sorry she left and it was all a big mistake.

I can't stand how her stuff is still here, either. Everywhere in the kitchen. Those little flowered plates she collected. Her recipes in a box, in her loopy handwriting, in purple pen. And the plaques with the quotes about living each day and finding joy and making lemonade out of lemons.

Those crooked ceramic animal sculptures Brett and I made in art. The dumb Happy Mother's Day card.

Doesn't she want any of it?

Dad puts some spaghetti onto my dish, then Brett's. "I have no idea if I cooked the noodles long enough, or if the meatballs have any taste," he says.

Brett looks at his plate. "The noodles are stuck together." He shoves some into his mouth. "And they're crunchy."

Dad sighs. "Then I definitely didn't cook them long enough."

So the three of us cut the crunchy noodles and eat the tasteless meatballs, and that's the only sound in the room.

BRIAN

It's the usual crazy Kowalski family Sunday dinner at our house. Dad's ranting about something with the government in Poland, Mom's telling everyone to eat, eat, eat, and my cousins—too many to name or count or even keep track of—are arguing, passing food, slapping each other on the back, and spitting (on purpose or accidentally, who knows).

I'm sitting next to Gram, who's chewing and staring at the wall. Mom says her mind's slowly turning into a pierogi.

All week Ethan's been obsessed with the desk-evator. It's all he can talk about. How the judges are gonna love it and kids will be able to stand at their desks anytime they want and this thing is gonna "take off."

But all I can think about is if I should ask Jamie out, and how I should do it. I mean, are we talkin' something casual, like *Hey, wanna go out?* or more serious, like, *Will you go out with me?* Big difference there, let me tell you.

And then what do I do if she says yes? Take her to a movie? Or the mall? Give her, like, a necklace or something? What do people actually do when they go out anyway?

I turn to Gram. "What do you think?"

She blinks.

"I think Jamie likes me. It's really hard to tell with her. She's nice to everyone. But she said I'm funny. She laughs at my jokes. She liked my sumo wrestler costume. That's something, right?"

I don't think Gram heard a word I said.

"I mean, how do you know if someone likes you?"

She keeps chewing. She's had that piece of chicken in her mouth for at least ten minutes.

"I have to break it to you, though, Gram. She's not Polish."

Gram raises her eyebrows, turns to me. "Not Polish?"

"Right. Sorry."

"You marry this girl?"

"No! I'm twelve, Gram. I'm not getting married anytime soon."

She wiggles her finger. "You listen to me, young man. Wait one hour before you go swimming."

Okay. Good to know.

She winks at me, then goes back to chewing the chicken.

ZOE

I tell Mom I can't take a break for dinner, and she brings a plate to my room. But I barely eat anything. This is too important. I'm online, reading every article I can find about invasive plant roots, and the clock is ticking.

We have ninety-six hours until Invention Day.

Can you imagine a world where we won't have to worry about native plant extinction? Where sensitive habitats are no longer threatened? Where biodiversity is restored to our planet?

My heart speeds up just thinking about the possibility.

A few years ago, in fourth grade, every class did a wax museum project. You had to choose an important figure from history and portray that person. Dress like him or her, and give a speech at our assembly as if you were that person.

I was Rachel Carson.

Not a lot of fourth graders knew who she was. Kids were choosing people like J. K. Rowling and Jackie Robinson and George Washington.

But Rachel Carson—she was one of the most famous women pioneers in the field of plant biology! She led a crusade to ban the awful pesticide DDT, and helped get the Environmental Protection Agency (commonly known as the EPA) created!

I mean, how much more important can you get?

I hope that one day, my name will be right alongside Rachel Carson's.

But for now, back to work.

ETHAN

The discussion of where the Marcus fam should go to dinner starts at about four thirty on Sunday, when my sister's getting hungry. (She claims she has a "small stomach.")

I say, pizza? Because that's what I always say. Mom says no, we had that last week.

She suggests Thai, but Dad says he's not in the mood for that. Then Dad says, "How about Mexican? I could go for an enchilada," but Erin shakes her head. "I don't want Mexican."

Then we all end up annoyed at each other.

It's a lot of fun.

Anyway, after like, ten other suggestions, Dad says he's making an "executive decision" and "let's go."

He takes us to this hot dog place where you park outside and shout your order into a speaker, and people bring the food to your car. The food delivery people are on roller skates, which is an added bonus. If I ever work at a restaurant, this would be my top choice.

Mom warns us that this isn't going to be a "regular thing."

Dad tells her to relax and live a little.

"Hot dogs aren't healthy, and we can only do this once in a while," she says.

Dad ignores her, bites into his dog, then closes his eyes and goes, "Ahhhhhh."

I'm in the backseat with Erin, ready for her usual Erin-ness, maybe some Spanish phrases thrown in, but she's acting weirdly normal. Even . . . nice?

"So how's your invention coming along?" she asks me. "You didn't quit?"

"Yeah, and we're done."

"Really? So you're ready for Thursday?"

"As ready as we'll ever be. How 'bout you and Zoe? What'd you decide?"

"Um . . . I think we're going to stick it out."

"Cool."

She shrugs. "Yeah, you know, sometimes things happen in mysterious ways."

"Right. They sure do."

I stuff some fries into my mouth. No doubt about it now. Erin definitely wrote the note that was in my locker. I don't know exactly why, because I never do with her, but I'm going to chalk it up to things like gravity and infinity and Mr. Delman's ties. You can't explain it, it just is.

ERIN

Zoe and I spent the entire weekend trying to re-create what happened with the roots. We mixed substances, tried them individually, even soaked the roots overnight. Nothing worked.

This kind of research, we both realized, could take years. Zoe said she's determined to get to the bottom of this and would report back when she found something out.

But I'm not sure we'll be able to uncover the mystery in time.

So I don't know what we should do, as far as Invention Day. We can't display a half-done project. An experiment without a solution. And, most importantly, no real invention.

We'd be disqualified. Embarrassed in front of everyone. And Marlon . . . I can't even bear to think about the conceited expression that'd be plastered on his face or what type of mean insult he'd hurl at me.

Only . . . this time I could be ready. This time, I could be prepared with a comeback.

I should do Invention Day for that reason alone.

That would actually be . . . hilarious.

CHAPTER THIRTY-ONE

Invention Day

ETHAN

The gym doors open at five p.m. for setup, even though Invention Day, which really should be called Invention Night, doesn't start until seven. There are posters all over McNutt about it, and families are invited.

Mom and Dad told me and Erin they're "bursting with pride" and "can't wait to see the soon-to-be-famous Marcus inventions."

This is turning out to be a pretty big deal.

So Brian and I, who are never early to anything, decide to get there right at five. I want to set up, then scope out the competition, and he wants to watch for Jamie. Dad drops us off with a thumbs-up and "See you later, boys!" Erin says Zoe's mom will take them a little later.

While we're waiting to check in with Gilardi, who's

sitting at a table outside the gym, I ask Brian if he knows for sure that Jamie's even coming.

"I heard her say she was."

"When?"

"Today, in LA. I was hanging around by her desk."

I shake my head. "You're obsessed, you know that?"

"Yeah. So?" He cranes his neck, searching the hallway. "What about it?"

We're one of the first groups in line, along with Parneeta, Naomi, and two guys who sit at the computer table in the cafeteria. Everyone's carrying their display board. Naomi also has a big plastic bin, and Parneeta's wheeling a cart loaded with boxes.

We're just holding our board and the desk-evator, which people are looking at kind of funny, like they can't figure out what it is. They'll see soon enough.

Once we get inside, Brian and I walk around the gym until we find the table with our names on it. It's right under the basketball net. Great spot! We stand up the display board on the table, lean the desk-evator against it, then stand back to see how it looks.

“Well, whaddya think?” I ask.

“Good, I guess.” Brian grins and jabs me. “No one will wonder if we made this ourselves, that’s for sure.”

“Remember, this is only a prototype,” I remind him. “An early design.”

“That it is.”

We both turn and scan the gym. And there are things going on that I couldn’t have imagined in my craziest dreams. Naomi smooths out a red tablecloth, then fills little bowls with candy and places them on her table. The computer guys are plugging in their laptops and firing them up. Another group is arranging balloons on their table and taping streamers around the edge. And Parneeta—get this—has a tall metal pole on a stand with a bright pink flag on top that says PARNEETA’S POUCHES.

What the heck?

“We’re idiots,” Brian says. “It’s confirmed. We’re complete idiots.”

I swallow a sudden lumpy throat ball. “Were we supposed to do all this? Like, decorate? Have bowls of candy? Was that on the form?”

“I don’t know! I didn’t go to Invention Day last year. I

guess this is a thing. How people get the crowd to come to their table." He smirks. "The judges, too, probably."

"That's not right. It shouldn't be about swag. And . . . tablecloths!"

"Face it, everything is. We're screwed." He glances toward the gym door. "Oh God, there's my mom. I told her not to get here this early."

Brian's mom waves excitedly, then walks over and hands Brian a plastic bag. "I thought you'd be hungry, honey. You too, Ethan. There's sandwiches, pretzels, and two clementines."

He takes the bag and throws it underneath our table. "Thanks. Now can you go and come back later, please? No other parents are here."

She winks and pinches his cheek. "Of course!"

After his mom leaves, Brian and I stand in back of our balloon-less, streamer-less, flag-less, candy-less table. And then, I swear, it's like I've stepped into the pages of *The Carrot Seed*. Only I have a desk-evator, not a carrot seed.

Naomi comes over, looks at our invention, tilts her head, and squints. "What is that?"

"It's a desk-evator," I say. "So kids can stand at their desks when they're tired of sitting and need to stretch their legs. You know, wake up their brains."

I demonstrate how the desk-evator folds in and out. Then I attach two of the chip clips to the edge of the table. "This will keep it on the desk. See?"

"Oh," she says. "Interesting. That's a lot of tape."

"Well, the thing is—" I start to explain.

She backs away, says she has to go. "Sorry, I have way more to set up."

Parneeta stops in front of us and bites her lip like she's trying not to laugh. The computer guys walk by and I hear one of them whisper, "They're so out of their league."

Romanov's parading around to each table with his arms crossed like he's sure he has everyone beat and why is anyone else even here. All that's on his table is the robotic hand and a black tablecloth. He doesn't even have a display board.

He stops in front of us, stares for about two seconds, then does that weird head shake, one slight right and one slight left. And leaves.

Everyone who sees the desk-evator seems to be saying, without saying it, that it's a joke. That we're a joke.

Brian picks up the plastic bag and looks inside, then takes out two sandwiches wrapped in plastic. He offers me one. "Turkey?" We sit on the floor behind our table.

"Should we go?" he asks, unwrapping his sandwich.

"What do you mean?"

"I mean, look at our invention. Look at our, uh, display. Maybe we should just sneak out the back and take the desk-evator with us."

"No! What do they know? It's the judges' opinions that count. And they'll get it, I'm sure they will. Even though it looks a little rough, they'll understand the concept."

"Okay, you keep the faith, man."

"So we didn't make a whole show of our table with balloons and stuff, but the main thing is that this is really important. The thousands of kids who get square butts in school every single day are counting on us. It's a good invention, I know it is."

"Yeah, yeah. You told me that a billion times." He takes a bite. "We probably should've gone with those hinges, though. The tape makes it look like crap."

I sigh. I can't eat. It's six thirty already, and every table is set up. Except one. I look around the gym and realize I don't see Erin and Zoe.

I get up and walk over to the empty table. It's theirs.

My sister would never be late to something like this. To anything.

What's wrong? Where are they?

CHAPTER THIRTY-TWO

To Be Continued

ERIN

Registration closes at six forty-five p.m. At exactly 6:42, Zoe and I walk through the front doors of McNutt. Ms. Gilardi's still at the table outside the gym. Perfect.

She stands and claps a hand across her heart when she sees us. "Oh, thank goodness you're here. I was starting to get concerned. The other groups have all checked in. Is everything okay?"

"Absolutely fine," I say.

She crosses our names off the list. "You better hurry inside and get set up."

"No worries." I open the gym door and motion to Zoe. We've got only two things to put on our table, so it won't take us very long.

When I get inside, it's exactly how I expected it to be. Like last year. Tables around the gym with everyone's inventions, plus signs, balloons, bright tablecloths, the works. Parneeta went all out. I'm not surprised. There's only one empty table, by the far end of the bleachers. Ours.

I turn to Zoe. "You okay with this?"

She nods. "I think it's very brave. And better than not showing up at all."

"Agree. All right, let's go."

On the way to our table, I catch Ethan's eye. He's got the desk-evator invention on his bare table with their display board. It looks like a little kid made it, compared to everyone else's professional-looking projects, but for some reason, I kind of like it.

Ethan's watching as I stand up our display board. Then Zoe places the one other item in front of it. It's a bleached-out root.

In a second, Romanov's here. As I knew he would be. He crosses his arms, quickly scans our board, then does this mean smirk. He turns to leave. But I'm ready.

"Marlon," I say. He turns back. "I'm not afraid to admit we struggled and have a long way to go. That's the sign of a great inventor."

Zoe holds up the root. "Edison, comma, Thomas."

"Japanese proverb," I add. "Fall down seven times, get up eight."

He laughs, rolls his head back. And then he walks away.

I squeeze my hands into fists and actually growl. I want the last word. "Excuse me!" I shout, but he doesn't stop.

Zoe puts her arm around my shoulders. "He's not worth it, Erin."

"But—"

"No. Don't stoop to his level. Stand tall. This is what we decided to do."

"You're right." My voice catches.

The gym doors are about to open for the families, but right before they do, Ethan and Brian come to our table.

Brian looks at our board, then claps twice. "Erin McBarren, gotta hand it to you. I couldn't have predicted this in a million years. It's actually kinda cool."

Ethan sighs. "You couldn't fix your project?"

"We could not," I answer. "We decided to go in another direction."

I reread our display board for the hundredth time.

The heading, in bubble letters: FAMOUS PEOPLE WHO FAILED AT FIRST.

We listed as many as we could fit on the board. Edison, Albert Einstein, Charles Darwin, Vincent van Gogh, Dr. Seuss, Walt Disney, Soichiro Honda, Abraham Lincoln, Steven Spielberg, even Lady Gaga and Jay-Z, who Zoe wanted to include so we could cover all fields. After their names, we have a short explanation of how each of them failed at some point.

But the best part is the entire right side of the board. It says ERIN MARCUS AND ZOE FELD-KRAMER.

After our names, we explained our experiment and our intended invention, the All-Natural Invasive Plant Destroyer. And then we wrote about how we made an accidental discovery, describing how something—and we will find out what—affected the root of an invasive plant. At the bottom, we have (also in bubble letters): TO BE CONTINUED.

You can never stop being optimistic about inventions. That's rule number one.

Ethan shoves his hands into his jean pockets. "It should say somewhere on there that this is all your brother's fault."

"Actually, it is," I say. "And it's okay." It's time to tell him.

"You didn't ruin our project," I confess. "When everything got messed up and spilled on the table, one of the substances, or a combination of them, changed some of the plant roots. But we didn't have enough time to find out which one. Or ones."

"Wait," Brian says. "Are you serious?"

"Yes."

"So"—Ethan points back and forth from himself to Brian—"let me get this straight. We kind of helped you? In an accidental-missed-catch kind of way?"

Zoe smiles and bobs her head just as the gym doors open. "You did! It was accidentally brilliant!" She touches his arm. "Like many inventions are."

"Wow." Ethan scans our display board. "I was inspired by Edison too. Kinda crazy, huh?"

I shrug. "Not so crazy." I see Mom and Dad, waving excitedly. "You guys better get back to your table."

"Hold on," Ethan says. "Come clean, Erin. You wrote the note, right?"

"What note?"

"About the folding table."

"I don't know what you're talking about."

"You didn't put a note in my locker?"

"No."

At that moment, out of the corner of my eye, I see the desk-evator collapse.

"Oh, Ethan," I groan. "You had to use TAPE?"

CHAPTER THIRTY-THREE

Panda-monium

ETHAN

Brian and I run to our table. The desk-evator has completely fallen apart. The spatulas got loose, and one of the chip clips somehow broke and tape is peeling everywhere. The whole thing just exploded. And of course, we forgot to bring an extra roll of duct tape.

Brian kicks the table and the display board falls over too. "This is a disaster. How are we supposed to fix this? We should just add our names to Erin and Zoe's fail list and call it a night."

In minutes the gym gets crowded, noisy, and hot. People are streaming in like this is the event of the century. Mom and Dad are heading toward Erin's table.

Brian stands up the board. I try retaping the spatulas, but the tape's lost its stickiness and they're not staying. The chip clip is busted. And the cutting board looks like it's about to break in half. So our invention is now basically a collection of random kitchen items and five pounds of useless tape.

"Forget it," Brian scoffs. "I told you weeks ago. Look at this place. We shouldn't even be here."

Romanov's demonstrating his robotic hand. Naomi's putting her antibiotic bandages on people's arms. The computer guys are . . . I don't even know what they're doing.

And Parneeta. She's next to us. Are you ready for this? A kid, who someone says is her little sister, is standing in front of the table in a panda costume, handing out samples of Parneeta's lightweight backpack invention. Why she's dressed as a panda, I don't know, but it's hard to resist a panda or a cute kid.

Little Panda Girl is stealing the show. People are lining up to get a sample and take a picture with her. They're putting on the backpacks like it's the greatest thing they've ever seen. Parneeta's Pouches are suddenly everywhere in the gym.

"I guess that's what you call marketing," Brian cracks.

Gilardi, standing on the first row of the bleachers,

taps on a microphone, and then it gets quiet. "Welcome, everyone! Isn't this wonderful? Aren't these kids amazing?" People clap and cheer. "In this room tonight might very well be a future entrepreneur or scientist or technical wizard." People clap again. And call out their kids' names.

Nobody calls out *Ethan* or *Brian*. Not even our own families.

"We will now begin the judging," Gilardi continues. "But I want to say congratulations to everyone, no matter whose invention wins! Please enjoy yourselves, and be sure to have some lemonade and cookies!"

She puts down the microphone, and then the judges start walking from table to table with clipboards. It's Gilardi and the other seventh- and eighth-grade science teachers, and for some reason, Mr. Delman. What an LA teacher would know about judging inventions, I have no idea. But I can pretty much guess we won't get his vote.

D'Antonio's here too, smiling and shaking the parents' hands, and Mean Secretary is parked on a chair at one end of the gym, eating cookies.

I turn to Brian. "What should we do?"

He shrugs. "Stand here and fake it?"

So we go behind our table and try to smile and act like we have a clue.

"I feel sick," I say.

Brian takes a step away. "Just don't puke on me, okay?"

Mom and Dad are hugging Erin. A Parenting 101 Success Story. The "rise above failure" lesson. Dad pats her on the back, and Mom takes a picture of her and Zoe in front of their display board while Erin holds up the plant root. Then they head toward me, along with Mr. Delman.

Delman gets there first. "Ethan, Brian," he says, tapping his pen on the clipboard and looking over what was once the desk-evator. "What do we have here?"

I pick up the cutting board and try to show him how it's supposed to work. "Uh, well, it kind of fell apart, but it's supposed to be this invention that will let kids stand at their desks. See, it unfolds, and you clip it onto the sides of your desk. . . ."

"Innovative," Dad comments. "I like it. Cutting-edge stuff here." He winks at me. "Get it? Cutting edge, cutting board."

"Stop," I mouth.

Delman writes something on his clipboard as Brian's mom appears with another plastic bag. "Dessert," she whispers. "From the bakery. The good one, by Uncle Mike's house."

Brian brushes his hand at her. "Any more questions, Mr. D? We'd be glad to answer them."

"Uh, no. Thank you. I have what I need." He moves on to the next table. Parneeta's.

Mom tilts her head. "I was wondering where my spatulas went. Well . . . this is certainly unique, I'll say that."

One by one, the other judges come to our table. And they all have pretty much the same reaction. Ranging from bad to horrible to complete stinkage. They don't say it. They're polite. But they don't have to. It's written all over their faces. And in the quick little scribbles on their clipboards before they happily move on to Parneeta.

I jab Brian. "We have to do something."

"Like what? Blow up the desk-evator in the middle of the gym?"

"Our invention might be a failure, but we don't have to be. And we can still get the message across."

"What are you talking about?"

I grin. "School got rules, that we know."

He grins back at me. "But McNutt number seven has got to go."

Then we shrug at each other, walk in front of our table, and go for it. The rap we did in my basement. What the heck at this point, you know?

We just start, and slowly a crowd forms around us. Kids, parents—even Little Panda Girl bounces over, giggling and dancing.

School got rules, that we know,
But McNutt number seven has got to go.
Sit, sit, sit, there goes your brain.
Sit some more, you go insane.
You know the deal, hours in a chair.
Then what happens, your butt gets square.
We gotta move, we gotta stand.
Hey, this ain't no joke, listen to our band.
It's time to make a change, it's time to be heard.
No more scomas, and that's the last word.

People applaud, cheer, whistle, and scream for more. Someone shouts, "Flash mob!" So we do the whole thing a second time, with the judges watching now. Then a third. Take that, Parneeta's Pouches! We're the Scomas, okay, and we can fire up the crowd too!

This is even better than doing the karaoke at Naomi's party. Maybe my future is in the entertainment industry, not the invention world. People are taking pictures and tweeting them—#sittingrap, apparently. This eighth-grade guy's taking video, and I hear him say this is the kind of thing that goes viral and he's posting it immediately.

After we finish and everyone claps again, it kind of breaks up. Before I even catch my breath, Zoe rushes up to me and throws her arms around my waist.

"I think your invention's great!" she cries. "And I think you're great!" She stands on her tiptoes, kisses me ON THE LIPS, then takes off and disappears into the crowd.

Whoa.

She kissed me. Zoe just kissed me?

I have no idea what to do. I'm sort of frozen. Did anyone see that? Where's Erin? Can't find her. Where did Zoe go? Don't see her. Where's Brian? He's standing next to Jamie. He's talking. She's not. He reaches for her hand, but she takes a step back. Oh no.

“Hello? Everyone, may I have your attention?” Gilardi has the microphone again. “The judges have come to a decision!”

The gym gets real quiet. Jamie walks away from Brian. Romanov pushes toward Gilardi on the bleachers. Little Panda Girl is asleep on the floor under Parneeta’s table.

Gilardi holds up some ribbons. “It’s getting late, so without further ado, here are the winners! In third place, Naomi Berland for her antibiotic bandage invention!” Everyone claps as Naomi comes forward and Gilardi hands her a ribbon.

“In second place, Veronica Lee for her innovative solar energy panel invention.”

Veronica gets her ribbon too.

“Now I know you’re all on the edge of your seats, but before I announce our winner, the judges have decided to award a special honorable mention this year. For the invention that shows the most promise, to Erin Marcus and Zoe Feld-Kramer, for their All-Natural Invasive Plant Destroyer. We can’t wait to see you back here next year!”

I don't know where Zoe is, but I see my sister's mouth drop open. Everyone applauds. Me included.

Gilardi asks the crowd to quiet down. "And our winner—drum roll please—is Parneeta Johar, for Parneeta's Pouches!"

Wild applause and cheering as Parneeta walks toward Gilardi to accept the first-place ribbon and a trophy. She bows, and her parents take forty gazillion pictures of her.

"We will be submitting Parneeta's invention for a US patent!" Gilardi says.

Erin marches over to Romanov. They're both close to me. "Marlon," I hear her say. "Isn't this interesting? All the winners—including the special honorable mention—are women."

He stamps his foot, turns, and shoves through the crowd. A few minutes later, the gym door slams.

Someone says, "I heard Romanov got disqualified!"

This other kid goes, "Why?"

"Stupidest thing. He blew off the display board."

Then it's basically this crazy stampede of people

packing up their stuff and congratulating Parneeta and parents telling their kids to hurry up. A few people slap me on the back and tell me the rap was sweet and excellent and so right.

Brian's slumped on the floor by our table. He doesn't look too good. Like the time he threw up on the roller coaster. "Jamie turned me down, man. Friend-zoned me. It was horrible. The worst moment of my life."

"What happened?"

He blows out a long breath. "I finally asked her out, okay? She said I'm cute and funny and she likes me. But she said it like I'm a cuddly stuffed animal or something. Then she told me she just started going out with Armando. I didn't know."

"Armando?"

"Mr. Potato Head."

"What?"

"At Naomi's Halloween party."

"Oh, him?"

"Yeah. So my heart is officially broken. Just thought you should know."

"Really sorry." I put the remains of the desk-evator

into one of the plastic bags that Brian's mom brought. "You okay?"

"Would you be okay after your heart was smashed into a hundred pieces?"

"Hey, they'll probably break up in a week and you'll get another shot."

He shakes his head, stands, grabs the display board. "Let's get out of here."

We meet my parents outside the gym. "I think you did a great job," Mom says. "We're very proud of you. We loved the rap song! It was adorable."

Dad gives me a thumbs-up.

And as we walk out the door into the parking lot, I'm expecting to see Zoe, or Erin, or even the US patent people waiting to sign up Parneeta. But who I see is Wesley, standing in back of some bushes by the front sidewalk, leaning against a brick wall, looking at me.

CHAPTER THIRTY-FOUR

How Things Are

ERIN

As far as I'm concerned, Invention Day was a success.

We didn't win, of course. We couldn't have. But Romanov didn't win either. And we got an honorable mention!

Not that I'm happy he suffered a major disappointment and his dream of a repeat first place was crushed and he stormed out of the gym alone.

It would be so mean to think that, wouldn't it?

Okay, I admit it, I think that.

And I'm a little glad. Yes, all right, more than a little. I'm secretly thrilled. Serves him right, don't you agree? Yes, you do, admit it too.

Now Zoe and I have an entire year to work on our invention. And we'll come back next year, strong and ready to show everyone what we're made of.

Yeah, I heard she kissed my brother. Everyone heard. And Jamie friend-zoned Brian. Everyone heard that, too.

Between that, Parneeta's little sister, Romanov, and Ethan and Brian's rap, Invention Day turned into a bit of a free-for-all. Not at all how I expected it to be.

That's just how things are sometimes. You gotta go with it.

What?

Stop, okay. Just stop.

ZOE

What can I say, I got caught up in the moment. And what a moment it was! I can't even describe it. You'll just have to spontaneously kiss someone someday and see what it feels like, and then you'll know.

I've been wanting to kiss Ethan ever since that day in his garage when the quiz on my phone confirmed I was in love. While I was watching him do that funny rap song, I felt dizzy and off balance and a little crazy. His cuteness was just too much. I suddenly understood the true meaning of the word *swoon*.

I'm not embarrassed. And no, I'm not sorry. Sometimes

in life, you have to close your eyes and leap, you know?

The only thing is, now that I've leaped, I'm not sure what to do next.

Ethan hasn't done anything or said anything or even acknowledged the *K* in any way, so I'm not sure how he feels. Or if he ever wants to kiss me.

If you hear anything, can you let me know? Thanks a lot, that would be great.

WESLEY

I went to Invention Day, yeah. By myself. It wasn't easy, but I knew the wrestling guys wouldn't be there. I mostly hung out by these guys who invented a new kind of synthesizer. After a while, I asked them to show me how it works.

And you know what? They did.

CHAPTER THIRTY-FIVE

Tomatoes

ETHAN

And then it's over.

I wash the spoons and spatulas and put them back into the kitchen drawer, then throw away the broken cutting board, the chip clips, and the tape. Erin carefully packs up their stuff into a plastic bin—they'll be continuing to work at Zoe's house—and Dad carries the folding table down to the basement. Mom sweeps the floor, then pulls their cars into the garage.

It feels quiet, and clean. And sad.

On Monday I'm back in school, sitting at my desk with a square butt and a soupy brain and feet that refuse to wake up. After all this, after everything I went through, nothing's changed.

So much for believing in yourself and standing up

for something you care about. It's like everything never even happened.

Except for my two days of Internet fame. The rap video did go semiviral over the weekend and the tweets were retweeted a respectable number of times. People laughed, shared it, then went on to something else, which is how it goes.

When I get home after school, it's the same as always—Erin upstairs doing her homework, Mom's instructions for starting dinner, nothing good in the fridge.

This is my life.

I go outside for a while and shoot some baskets, but that doesn't cheer me up. I watch this little kid across the street ride his tricycle, but that doesn't make me feel better either. Then I go back inside and check the fridge again, and the pantry, and the freezer, for anything resembling a decent snack.

I find a lone root beer Popsicle in the way back of the freezer, buried under a package of peas. I almost feel happy, but when I unwrap it, half is crusted with ice and the rest is goopy and syrupy. I put it on the counter and stand there and watch it melt.

Erin walks into the kitchen and rips a banana off the bunch hanging by the sink. "What's the matter?"

"Nothing."

She peels the banana and takes a bite. "What are you doing with that Popsicle?"

I shrug. "Watching it die."

"Oh, okay."

"This whole thing . . . I don't even know anymore. That day, my protest, all I really ever wanted was to be able to stand at my desk. Then I got swept up in it. I mean, I started to believe my invention had a chance. That people would get it. And I could change things, you know?" I sigh. "McNutt number seven has got to go. . . ."

She nods. "I know the feeling."

"Anyway, it all was for nothing."

"Ethan, your idea wasn't bad. It has potential. You just needed to make it better. You should've used some other materials. Not a cutting board and chip clips—"

"I know, okay! I know." I throw the Popsicle into the sink. "That was stupid."

"Listen . . . I'm sorry it fell apart."

We look at each other.

"Thanks," I say.

She takes another bite, chews it five times. "Well."

Neither of us leaves.

I lean against the counter. "So you really didn't put a note in my locker?"

"I told you before, I don't know anything about a note. What did it say?"

"Someone was telling us to make the desk-evator more like a folding table. We'd been trying to make something that, like, raised up. Whatever. Maybe it was Zoe? She, uh, you know."

"Yeah. I heard. You . . . like her?"

All I can say is, "Uh . . ."

"It's all right. You don't have to tell me. I'll ask her about the note." Erin pulls her phone from her back pocket and starts tapping the screen. A few seconds later, she says, "It wasn't her."

"Ah, why does it matter? Invention Day is over. My life is over."

She laughs.

"Why are you laughing?" I groan. "It's not funny."

"I don't know, you almost sounded like . . . me."

"Oh God."

She rolls her eyes. "Really. That's scary."

I smile. "Hey, remember when we did that tomato protest? Now *that* was a protest."

"Yeah, it sure was. And it worked."

"I still won't eat tomatoes."

"Me either."

"Weird," I say. "Two peas in a pod?"

"How can we be? We're oil and water."

I nod. "Day and night."

She raises an eyebrow. "Up and down."

"Right."

"Well . . ." She takes a few steps toward the family room. "I have a lot of homework."

"Okay."

"Ethan . . . it'll be all right."

"You mean the desk thing?"

She shrugs. "That too."

CHAPTER THIRTY-SIX

The Real Protest

ETHAN

On Tuesday, when Brian and I get to LA, Delman's wearing a tie that says: NO QUESTION IS DUMB. Where does he get all these ties?

Brian jabs me. "Yeah, no question is dumb, except if I asked it." He walks down the middle row. Erin and Zoe come in, go to their desks. Ever since Invention Day, it's been really awkward whenever I see Zoe. I don't know what I'm supposed to do now or how to act around her.

Delman's straightening a pile of papers. He glances at me and I realize I'm still standing by his desk. "Something on your mind, Ethan?"

I should just go to my desk, right, and let the scoma take over like usual, because what other choice do I have? But suddenly it hits me that I do have another choice. Was that what Erin was trying to tell me? It'll be all right, but only if I keep trying to make it all right.

"Yeah, Mr. Delman, there is something on my mind."

"Yes?"

I point to his tie. "I have a question."

"Sure. We have a minute or so before the bell rings."

"You remember my invention? The desk-evator?"

He half smiles. "Hard to forget it."

"I was wondering. You think I could use something like that in here? When I just need to stand for a while? Take a break from sitting?"

He shakes his head. "I understand how you're very passionate about this issue, and that's certainly admirable. But I'm afraid you'd block Naomi. She wouldn't be able to see the whiteboard."

"Not if we didn't sit in rows."

He raises his eyebrows. "Excuse me?"

"I mean, maybe we could rearrange the desks in, like, a circle?"

"They're fine how they are, Ethan. I like rows. Thank you for the suggestion, though."

"But—"

The bell rings. "Now, if you'll take your seat," he says.

I trudge to my desk. Delman tells us to take out the short story we started yesterday.

My sister looks at me.

I drop into my chair.

"All right, everyone," Delman says. "Let's get started."

Suddenly Erin bolts from her seat and stands next to her desk. Straight and tall, hands on her hips. It gets real quiet. Everyone stares at her. What the heck is she doing?

"Erin?" Delman asks.

"Mr. Delman, I have a question too."

He tilts his head. "Yes?"

"Whoever said that learning had to be done in a chair?"

A few people in the back laugh.

"No, I'm serious," Erin says. "Who decided that once you get to junior high, you have to sit at a desk all day?"

Delman crosses his arms. "We're not going to get into this right now. Please take your seat."

She doesn't.

"Did you know," she asks, "a recent study found that walking can greatly improve creativity? And a different study found that when students take breaks and move around, they stay focused and actually perform better?"

Delman narrows his eyes. "Miss Marcus. This isn't the time."

"Yes, it is!" She looks around the room, then waves her arms. "Get up, everyone! Remember the sit-ins from the sixties?"

People look confused, and like they don't want to get into trouble.

Erin stamps a foot. "Come on! We learned about them last year in social studies! The lunch counter in North Carolina? Well, this is a stand-in! A real protest. We should have a voice."

Brian goes, "Yeah!" and jumps up. Then Zoe does too. They both stand next to their desks.

I stare at Erin.

"Ethan," she says, "get up! This is for you!"

It's like she's me and I'm her. Is this really happening, or is it a movie where we magically switched places?

She smiles. "Tomatoes."

I nod. Tomatoes. I push myself out of my chair and stand. One by one, everyone else in the room stands too. Not one kid is sitting. I have to say, it's pretty amazing.

“Should we do the rap?” Brian cracks, and someone goes, “Yeah, do it!”

“All right,” Delman says. “Enough. If you don’t sit at your desks right now, I’ll have no choice but to write all of you up and send you to Mrs. D’Antonio’s office. Is that what you want?”

Erin holds up the short story we’ve been reading. “No. We want to express our opinion, Mr. Delman. We’re taking a stand. Like in this story, when they went on strike for better working conditions. I don’t believe we’re asking for too much here.”

If Erin runs for president one day, which I have no doubt she’ll do, I’ll vote for her.

Delman’s silent for a few seconds. He looks around like he’s weighing his options.

I clear my throat. “Okay, I think we’ve made our point.” I sit in my chair and motion for everyone else to sit too. They do. Everyone except Erin.

“Are you willing to listen to us?” she asks.

He sighs. “Come and talk to me after class, Miss Marcus.”

Erin nods, then sits and pushes up her mechanical pencil like it’s any other day.

Delman loafer-taps down my aisle, like it's any other day. "Now, let's get back to the story at last. Who can summarize the overall theme?"

Erin's hand shoots up. No one else is volunteering.

Delman smiles. "Yes, Erin, I'm sure you have a thought."

She clasps her hands. "I do. See, the two sides started out very far apart. Different things were important to them. *They* were different. They didn't understand each other. I mean, isn't that why people don't like each other? But then, once they started talking, and negotiating, they had more in common than they realized. Each side had to compromise before any real work could be accomplished."

"Excellent," Delman says. "I couldn't have said it better myself."

I raise my hand.

"Ethan? You have something to add?"

"Uh, yeah, I just wanted to say that Erin really helped me get this story. So, thanks."

"You're welcome," she says. "Anytime."

Delman looks at her, then me. "Okay, let's continue."

Like it's any other day.

CHAPTER THIRTY-SEVEN

Rin

ERIN

As soon as class ends and everyone clears out (except for my brother, hanging around by the bulletin board), I approach Mr. Delman. He starts to speak, but I hold up a hand. "If I can explain."

"Certainly," he says. "Go ahead."

"If you need to give me Reflection for starting the stand-in, I'll accept it with no arguments. But you said yourself that we've done badly on the last few quizzes and the unit test. I mean, not me, but many others."

"That's correct."

"So what would it hurt to try something different? Think outside the box. See if standing, or moving, or taking stretch breaks even, can improve students' performance. If not, then no harm, go back to the old way."

He tips his head. "Are you planning a career as an attorney, Erin?"

"Oh, I haven't decided. There are many careers I'm considering. I'm good at a lot of things." I turn to Ethan. "Anything you'd like to add?"

He grins. "I think you covered it."

Mr. Delman picks up his briefcase from the floor and starts putting papers into it. "Well, I'll tell you what. I'll take this under advisement."

"What does that mean?" Ethan asks.

"It means I'll give it some thought."

"Thank you," I say, then motion to Ethan. I go out and he follows. You have to know when to make your exit. That's crucial.

"Whoa," he says, and I put my finger over my lips. Mr. Delman could still hear us. Ethan and I can talk later. We quietly walk down the hallway toward our lockers.

I didn't plan this, if that's what you're wondering. Not until the moment I overheard Ethan asking Mr. Delman if he could use the desk-evator in class. Then I knew I had to do something to help him. I mean, I wanted to. And also, I knew if I pulled it off right, I wouldn't get in trouble.

Even if I did, it would've been okay. There's a first for everything. And besides, this was important. In so many ways.

ETHAN

So that's how you work within the system. That's how you get rules to change.

Erin looks at the time on her phone. "Oh, I've missed the bus! And it's an hour until the late bus."

"So you'll walk."

"It's cold out."

"It's fine."

"You'd still be wearing shorts if Mom didn't make you wear jeans."

"True."

We open our lockers, grab our backpacks, load them up, and walk out the front doors together. Erin pulls on a knitted hat and gloves, then wraps a scarf around her neck.

"Seriously," I say, "it's not that cold."

"What are you talking about! It's freezing!"

After we cross the street and we're in the park, I say, "Thanks, Rin."

She looks at me and smiles. "You're welcome."

Rin. My first word.

Mom likes to tell random strangers how I didn't talk for the longest time when I was little and they were worried about me. Then one day I just said my sister's name. Or part of it. Which assured them I was brilliant, and besides, it was *so* cute. People usually have a story about their own kid or someone else's, who also didn't talk and is now an astrophysicist or something. So maybe my future is bright, who knows.

"That was amazing," I say. "A stand-in? Only you would come up with that."

"I know." She laughs. "Just kidding. Sort of."

"I can't believe you did that. Stood your ground and protested. Got everyone else to do it too. Then explained it all rationally to Delman."

"Hey, I can live on the edge if I want to." She pulls down her hat, then stuffs her hands into her pockets.

"You sure can."

Yeah, that's my sister, living on the edge, bundled up with only her eyes and nose showing. The kind of edge that gets things to happen.

"Can I ask you something?" I say.

"Okay."

"When you told me you didn't think I could do it—make the desk-evator—that I didn't have what it takes—were you saying that because you wanted me to keep trying?"

She peers at me from under the hat. "What do you think?"

"I think yes."

"We'll leave it at that, then." She strides ahead.

We're almost through the park when I realize Wesley's sitting on the bench where the seagulls usually are, but there aren't any. They're gone. He's by himself. I can only see his profile, but he looks different. Not as scary.

Then, I just know. I don't know how, I just do. It was him.

CHAPTER THIRTY-EIGHT

Spaghetti, Take Two

WESLEY

The day before Mom left, she dropped one of the little flowered plates when she was dusting it, and it broke into a bunch of jagged, sharp pieces. She started crying. She couldn't stop crying. It was just her and me in the kitchen. And I said, in this mean voice, "It's just a plate, Mom, get over it."

I didn't know. I thought she was crying about the plate.

For a long time, I thought that her leaving had something to do with what I said. But I guess it's what Gilardi explained—Mom wasn't happy with her life here. Maybe it didn't have as much to do with me as it did with her.

Dad, Brett, and I are in the kitchen for what Dad's calling "Spaghetti, Take Two." He brings a bowl to the table. "Here we are," he says.

Here we are is right. This is it. This is how it is and how it's gonna be from now on.

Dad takes some garlic bread from the oven, slices it, then puts the pieces on a tray and brings it to the table. Brett's bent over his dish, shoveling spaghetti into his mouth. He doesn't talk when he eats, and there's sauce on his chin. That's how it is too.

"How does it taste?" Dad asks Brett.

"Not as crunchy."

Dad laughs as I try the spaghetti. "Well?" he says.

"It's pretty good," I say.

Dad glances at Brett, who's attacking a piece of garlic bread like it's an opponent he's ripping to shreds. Dad looks at me and shrugs, like he's saying the same thing. This is how it is and how it's gonna be. I get this feeling he's telling me he agrees it sucks that she left, but we gotta find a way to make it work and be okay.

Brett does this multilevel burp, thumps his chest with his fist, then looks up. "What?"

Dad grins.

"What're you lookin' at me for?" Brett says. "It had to come out."

"More spaghetti?" Dad asks, pushing the bowl in his direction.

"Yeah, sure. You guys are so frickin' weird sometimes."

"What's wrong with that?" I say.

Dad says, "Nothing. Nothing at all."

CHAPTER THIRTY-NINE

Last Words

BRIAN

It took me a few days, but I'm over it, I swear. Jamie and Armando are a thing and that's that. I saw them holding hands. I saw them kissing. I knew she was a long shot for me. Armando's really tall.

Anyway, we changed seats in math and Veronica Lee's at my table. We've been talking. About math problems, mostly. She's kind of cute, don't you think?

She's also not Polish. Please don't mention that to Gram. Because she keeps asking Mom if I've set a date. She also accused me of stealing her socks.

I must've told her I didn't take them, like, ten times.

Finally she seemed to believe me. "Well, if they're gone," she said, "it must be a blessing in disguise."

"Gram," I answered. "I think everything is."

ZOE

I worked up my courage and asked Ethan if he wanted to go to a movie with me this weekend. He said, and I quote, "Okay."

Okay!

OKAY!

Did you ever hear such a stupendous word in your life?

WESLEY

This time, when Dad offers me the phone, I take it.

It's good to hear her voice.

ERIN

I'm preparing a report and PowerPoint for Mrs. D'Antonio on the sitting/standing/desk issue. I think she'll find it very informative.

And I think we can really make some changes at McNutt.

I would've been fine with the way things were, but okay, I'll just say it. It's not always about me.

ETHAN

"Just as the little boy had known it would."

With a little help from his sister.

The sister part isn't in *The Carrot Seed*.

That's in my story.

ACKNOWLEDGMENTS

I HAVE NEVER INVENTED ANYTHING, UNLESS you count the retainer I made out of a paper clip when I was in middle school. (My best friend had gotten a retainer, which I thought was very cool, and—what can I say—I wanted to be cool too.) But even so, I believe that inventors have something in common with writers. We both begin with the same thing—an idea. When you first come up with it, you don't quite know if it's brilliant or ridiculous or crazy. Depending on the day or the angle of the sun, you might think one of those, or all three.

I have many people to thank for loving the idea for this book (and not thinking it was ridiculous or crazy): my patient and wise agent Alyssa Eisner Henkin, who kept the faith with me through eleven drafts and never let me give up; my perceptive editor, Fiona Simpson, and the team at Aladdin for their support, guidance, and insightful advice; and Laura Lyn DiSiena and Hugo Santos for their terrific cover design. Gracias to Gillie

Adler for the Spanish assistance. And to my friends and family—especially Ben, Rachel, Sam, and Cassie—you continue to amaze me with your unending encouragement and love. A book doesn't become a book without these essential ingredients. My last thank you is for you. Readers simply rock the world. But you knew that, didn't you? Rock on.

What's next for Ethan and the gang?

READ AN EXCERPT FROM *ETHAN MARCUS MAKES HIS MARK* TO FIND OUT.

ETHAN

As worst days go, the Monday after Thanksgiving break is right up there with the last day of summer vacation. Not as bad, I'll give you that. But hear me out. The alarm goes off at seven fifteen. You jolt awake, and then three sad facts slowly materialize in your brain: (1) The little party you had going on in the family room with constant televised sports and unlimited snacks is over. (2) Three months of winter are ahead. No more wearing shorts, shooting baskets on the driveway, or going outside without a jacket. And (3) School. You have to go back.

Enough said? Yeah, I thought so.

On top of that, you're still recovering from Thanksgiving itself. The stuffing-related stomachache, your relatives interrogating you, and having to sit next to

Grandpa Jerome, who kept yelling "WHAT?" while spitting half-chewed turkey on your arm. Luckily, you had a fancy cloth napkin to use as a shield.

Unfortunately for me, today is that Monday.

I drag myself out of bed and grab a T-shirt and jeans from the pile of clothes on my beanbag, then go downstairs to the kitchen, where my sister, Erin, is spreading peanut butter on a piece of toast. Perfectly even, making sure to completely cover each corner.

She sighs. "I thought this day would never come. I'm so happy to be going back to school. Being home gets really old after a while."

I make a grumble/growl noise because words are just too much effort at the moment.

She cuts her toast into six equal squares, then pops one into her mouth. She chews it exactly five times before swallowing. She's very precise about chewing. And everything else.

I stumble to the cabinet, take out a bowl, plunk it on the counter.

"I'm so excited to start the historical-fiction unit in language arts," Erin says. "I heard we get to dress up as our favorite character at the end. How fun will that be?"

I get the cereal, milk, a spoon. "I can't think of anything I want to do more."

She rolls her eyes, then smiles. "Oh, Ethan."

Erin's only eleven months older than me, and we're both in seventh grade, but she's sounding more and more like Mom every day. This is not good on a lot of levels.

I stand at the counter, hunch over my bowl, start eating.

Erin finishes her toast, then rinses the dish and knife and puts them into the dishwasher. She hoists her backpack onto a stool and rifles through it. "Wow, this is *so* unlike me. Good thing I checked. I almost forgot my mechanical pencil! I think I left it in my room. Be back in a sec." She runs out of the kitchen.

I keep eating my cereal, but even Cheerios aren't cheering me up.

When Erin comes back, I ask, "Where's Mom?" Dad leaves for work at five a.m., so he's never around in the morning, but Mom usually is.

"She had to run out early for a staff meeting. I assured her we'd lock up." Erin glances at me. "You better get moving. The bus will be here in . . ." She checks the time on her phone because she doesn't trust the clock on the microwave. "Ten minutes."

I scoop up the last soggy circle, then put my bowl into the sink.

Erin tilts her head. "Dishwasher."

I groan but open the dishwasher door and put my bowl and spoon inside. After everything that happened with Invention Day a few weeks ago, Erin and I have a different kind of deal going on. A sort of peace-ish treaty. We get how the two of us are day and night and black and white and all that. But that doesn't mean we don't still annoy each other. Fairly frequently.

"Where's your backpack?" she asks.

I look around the kitchen. "Upstairs?"

"Were you planning on getting it anytime soon?"

As I was saying.

A few minutes later I have my backpack and we're out the door, with Erin checking that it's locked about ten times. She even goes, "Okay, okay, the door is locked."

"Yes! It's locked!" I pull her arm. "Let's go."

At the bus stop, most people's eyes are half-closed,

and some kids are swaying a little, like they're asleep while standing on the sidewalk. When the bus gets there, I take my usual seat next to Brian Kowalski.

He grunts.

I yawn.

We understand each other perfectly, and have since kindergarten.

People are quiet during the ride, and I know for certain that every single kid on this bus is dreading the first sight of McNutt Junior High. Every kid except one. Erin's in the front row talking to Parneeta, who's definitely asleep. Eyes closed, head plastered to the window, mouth slightly open. But that doesn't stop Erin from describing in great detail the "supposedly riveting" historical-fiction book we're going to read in LA.

Too soon, it's 8:20 a.m., first period, and I'm in math with my butt planted in a chair. Mrs. Genovese peers at us through her giant round owl glasses and grins. "Welcome back, everyone!" She gestures to the whiteboard. "Let's get right down to work. Go ahead and start the warm-up problems. I hope your brains aren't still full of turkey!"

Mine obviously is. I forgot my pencil case in my locker and have to raise my hand to ask for a pencil. Mrs. Genovese has an emergency stash for people like me. Nice, but if you don't return the pencil, sharpened, at the end of class, she writes your name in a little notebook. It affects your grade in some way. It's happened. I've heard.

She hands me a pencil, and I stare at the first problem. I've also forgotten how to do any kind of equation. How many days until winter break? Fifteen. Correction: fifteen long, boring, scoma-inducing seven-hour days of school.

Yeah, I'm still having scomas. Scoma = school-coma, in case you forgot. After making the desk-evator for Invention Day, I had high hopes. The concept was brilliant—it really was. Even if the prototype was made from spatulas, chip clips, a broken cutting board, and an entire roll of duct tape. Don't ask.

My plan—my dream—was that kids would clip it onto their desks and be able to stand up in class when they needed to stretch their legs and defog their brains. It didn't win or anything, but afterward, Erin got people to do a serious protest in LA about how long we have to sit in school. The protest was amazing—everyone did it! We've—uh, she's—been working on a report about the benefits of standing desks, and we're going to present it to Mrs. D'Antonio, the principal, but until then my butt remains sadly in my seat.

I was sure I'd be scoma-free by now, but Erin says there are a lot of "facts and figures" to "compile" and she's been "really busy." Busy with what, you want to know? Busy being Erin.

I squint at the whiteboard and try to remember what a polynomial is, then look out the window for help. Sometimes that works. Like the sun pierces my brain or something. But instead I see something better than help. A big, fat snowflake drifting past the glass.

A minute later I spot a second one. Then a third, a fourth, and, suddenly, a bunch more falling from the whitish-gray sky.

This is good. Definitely good.

A blizzard is supposed to hit some parts of the Midwest today. The weather people are calling it Frankenstorm. But last night Mom and Dad weren't buying it. Dad packed up his work papers like usual. "They often blow these things out of proportion," he said. Mom agreed and told us to plan on going to school since it hadn't been canceled.

Mom and Dad are not panicky-type people. They always stick to their Parenting 101 philosophy: stay calm, be patient, and let your kids make their own choices. Except, apparently, in the case of snow predictions. Because I would've decided to stay home. You know, just as a precaution.

When math is over, I give Genovese the pencil so she won't write my name in her pencil-criminal notebook, and then I go to social studies. It keeps snowing. Science. More snow. By now nobody's concentrating or even listening. The view out the window is hypnotizing us.

People are whispering and sneak-texting under their desks. A rumor starts floating around about an early dismissal. And another rumor that tests are going to be moved back and homework deadlines will be extended.

In Spanish, Señora Pling is more jittery than usual, her bracelets jangling wildly as she sweeps her arm toward the window, shouting, *"¿Qué pasa?"*

Then the best rumor of all hits the McNutt hallways: not only an early dismissal, but a possible snow day tomorrow. Everyone's saying it's supposed to keep snowing all night. I hear eight inches. Ten. Twenty! A hundred!

Zoe Feld-Kramer, Erin's best friend, rushes up to me as I'm walking into the cafeteria for lunch. She grabs my hand and squeezes it because I think she thinks we're going out. "Maybe if there's a snow day, we can have plans!" she says. "Hang out? Do something fun?"

I clear my throat. "Uh . . . maybe."

She zooms toward the table where she sits with Erin and the rest of their friends.

At Invention Day, Zoe kissed me. Yes, on the lips. We went to a movie once. Just her and me. It was a dumb movie and Dad drove us and the whole deal was really awkward, and now I have no idea about anything.

"Marcus!" Brian calls, waving at me. "Get over here!"

I haven't even unwrapped my sandwich when Mrs. D'Antonio's voice crackles over the loudspeaker. "May I have your attention please?"

The cafeteria is 100 percent silent. People are holding their water bottles in mid-drink. Forks and spoons are down; eyes are wide. No one's even blinking. It's like a sitting freeze dance.

"Due to the snow, we will be dismissing . . ."

And it's official. We're getting out of here at two p.m. Mrs. D says more, but I can't hear because the cafeteria more or less explodes. The guys at my table stand and applaud. The theater table starts singing a song from *Wicked*, I think. The people at the popular-kid table are taking pictures and immediately posting them (#mcnuttearlydismissal, of course). Brian throws his banana high into the air, then catches it behind his back with one hand. Mrs. Hinkley points at him and blows her whistle. She's blowing her whistle at everyone.

I want to jump and high-five the cafeteria window, but Hinkley'll nail me. So I shout, "Thank you, Frankenstorm!" For saving my sad, scomatized butt and turning an absolute worst day into an absolute best day.

ERIN

This is terrible.

I know, okay? I know what you're thinking. How could I not be happy about an early dismissal and potential snow day? The thing is, and maybe I'm in the minority here, but I like school. Actually, I *love* school, and I'm not embarrassed about saying it. Always have, always will.

Each year, when I tear open the new school-supply pack Mom orders from the PTO, I'm in heaven. There's nothing in the world like six beautiful blank spiral notebooks and the anticipation of filling them with my neat, organized notes all year long. The scent of the clean, fresh paper gets me every time! I use index cards too—for studying and review—and thankfully, a package of five hundred is always included in the box.

I was *so* looking forward to discussing the periodic table in science. I studied it all during break, so I was well prepared. And in LA, Mr. Delman was going to distribute the new novel and read the first chapter aloud. We were supposed to begin talking about point of view and fact versus opinion!

But instead, at 2:01 p.m., what am I doing? Trudging to my locker, putting everything into my backpack, and filing out the back door toward the buses.

Now it'll be another long, slow afternoon at home,

trying to find things to do. I was already going stir-crazy over Thanksgiving break. I completed a one-thousand-piece puzzle, watched movies, finished two books, even reorganized all my dresser drawers. And, of course, continued my research for the report on standing desks.

When I have lots of assignments and projects for my classes, my heart just feels happier. If I can get into bed with everything crossed out in my assignment notebook, I know I'll sleep well.

Brian and Ethan are in line at our bus, doing the breaststroke as if they're swimming through the blizzard. I stand behind them, and in a few seconds my hat and backpack straps and jacket are covered with snow.

"We might not make it out alive!" Brian shouts.

Ethan laughs. "Every man for himself!"

My brother picks up a handful of snow and plops it onto Brian's back. Brian whoops, then does the same thing to Ethan. At least the two of them have the sense not to walk home like they usually do. It actually does look kind of bad—I can hardly make out Zoe waiting in her bus line. Still, I don't see why we couldn't have gotten through the last two periods of the day.

I settle into my regular seat behind the driver and next to Parneeta, who's got a huge smile on her face. "Isn't this excellent?" she says. "As soon as I get home, I'm catching up with all my favorite beauty blogs. There's usually a ton of new posts on Mondays."

I hold my backpack on my lap. "We're going to have to make up what we missed, you know. An extra day in June, I'm sure."

"So? Who cares!"

The bus is louder than normal—everyone's talking and shouting and throwing crumpled wads of paper. The driver, Joe, isn't even telling us to "dial it down a notch" like he usually does. He's singing and drumming his fingers on the steering wheel.

Finally we start moving. My phone buzzes, and I pull it out of my backpack. Text from Zoe: If there's a snow day tomorrow, maybe we can all hang out.

By "all" she means Ethan.

Maybe, I reply.

Maybe?

I should probably review some math problems, I say. And I'm still working on the report for Mrs. D'Antonio.

Erin! Snow days are a gift! You have to do something fun on a snow day. It's a law. She sends me a bunch of smiling emojis. And snowflakes.

Ha-ha. I'll think about it.

Zoe has decided she's in love with my brother. I told her I'm okay with it, but the truth is, just between you and me, I'm trying but I don't exactly see it. He has some charm, and can be funny in a sloppy-clueless way, and I guess a lot of girls think he's cute. And don't get me wrong, I want my best friend to have some romance in her life. But you can't let love take over everything else. Besides, what do they even have in common? I mean, Zoe's not even focusing on the Be Green Club anymore! That was everything to her prior to the Invention Day kissing incident.

The bus crawls along. What's normally a twenty-minute trip takes twice the amount of time. Finally we reach our stop and I get off, along with Ethan and some other kids. My brother and I clomp through the snow toward our house. The streets are barely plowed, and icy pellets are pinging my face. Unpleasant. Aggravating. Just, ugh.

"Isn't this awesome!" Ethan grins, kicking piles of snow as we walk. His jacket's not even zipped.

Now it's me who grunts, like he did this morning. "I'd rather be at school."

"You're crazy!" Ethan shouts, then clomp-runs the rest of the way home.

Maybe. But he's crazier.